LOBSTER LAND

LOBSTER LAND

SUSAN
CARLTON

HENRY HOLT AND COMPANY

New York

Thanks all around . . . to Kate Farrell, wise, wry, and perceptive at the meta and micro level (the specifics of paint gallons and prophylactic packaging come to mind), and to Robin Tordini, ever-charming and capable; to Rosemary Stimola, a marvelously enthusiastic agent; to Martha Rich, for her stupendous illustration; to the Monday morning writers' group, especially Carol Lee Lorenzo; to Coco Myers, my doppelganger, and Carol Eisenberg, who walks the walk; to my parents, for their heart, spirit, and infectious optimism; to Ralph Carlton, my actual, factual true love; and, of course, to Annie and Jane Carlton, for every little thing and for everything.

JF Carlton
Carlton, Susan R. S. K.,
 1960-
Lobsterland

Henry Holt and Company, LLC
Publishers since 1866
175 Fifth Avenue
New York, New York 10010
www.HenryHoltKids.com

Henry Holt® is a registered trademark of Henry Holt and Company, LLC.
Text copyright © 2007 by Susan Carlton
All rights reserved.
Distributed in Canada by H. B. Fenn and Company Ltd.

Library of Congress Cataloging-in-Publication Data
Carlton, Susan R. F. K.
Lobsterland / Susan Carlton.—1st ed.
p.   cm.
Summary: Sixteen-year-old Charlotte wants nothing more than to escape
the tiny island off the Maine coast where she has spent her life, and so she works on
applications to boarding schools while wondering if her parents and young siblings are
ready for her to leave, or she is ready to leave her life-long boyfriend.
ISBN-13: 978-0-8050-8096-4 / ISBN-10: 0-8050-8096-1
[1. Interpersonal relations—Fiction.   2. Family life—Maine—Fiction.
3. Islands—Fiction.   4. Self-realization—Fiction.   5. Maine—Fiction.]   I. Title.
PZ7.C216853Lob 2007   [Fic]—dc22   2006037745

First Edition—2007 / Designed by Laurent Linn
Printed in the United States of America on acid-free paper. ∞

1   3   5   7   9   10   8   6   4   2

To r.k.c.—
love of my island(s)

Wisdom comes with winters.

—*Oscar Wilde*

MONDAY

One (a)

Put yourself in my shoes. Specifically, olive green stilettos, size five and a half. Now bolt for the 3:35 ferryboat home, home being an iceberg a blink away from Portland, Maine. Oh, and it's December so the streets are gripped with ice. Push a stroller with one hand (little brother) and pull a radiant child with the other (little sister). Pass random tourists who are drinking in the view, a sign of idiocy if you ask me. If these sightseers walked my walk—running in heels to the ferry, dropping the siblets at day care, slogging through tenth-grade ridiculousness, reclaiming said siblets, busting ass, still in heels, back to the ferry—they'd know the truth.

It's all about making the fugging boat.

The island has a real name, but I call it Bleak. Hello, Bleak.

At the mouth of the pier, next to the giant tin can of a ferry, I see Noah. He's my first: friend (age zero), kiss (age six), stitches (a hockey brawl, age nine), spin-the-bottle (age eleven), mutual grope (age thirteen), love of life (age thirteen to the still-virginal present). We've been inseparable for sixteen of our sixteen years.

He bends down to give me a fast kiss. "Came to tell you I'm not getting on."

I take the Mainely Java coffee cup from his hands and gulp. It's lukewarm.

"I'll try to catch the 5:10," he says. "Promised Susannah I'd help her with vocab."

"Over macchiatos?" Susannah is my bestish friend, but suddenly she's all oh-help-me-study, Noah.

He shrugs. His hair jangles against his shoulders.

I lean in for a more gratifying kiss, but the air horn bleats from the boat's bridge, three stories up. I've heard the blast twice a day since birth—11,819 times, give or take. Even so, it makes me jump. I fall sideways off my shoe.

"Later," I yell to Noah. But he's already out of earshot. I'm stuck holding his backwash.

I run down the wide metal plank that swallows cars into the belly of the boat, the siblets in tow. My backpack weighs me down—with work, with guilt. With, specifically, applications to boarding schools. From this minute forward I have ninety-seven hours—until Friday at 5 P.M.—to apply to schools in other, more glamorous

4

states, where I'm not surrounded by dreary water or, presumably, idiots on all sides.

Today at lunch I skipped the cafeteria and slipped over to the Portland post office to pick up the mail. Our island is so, well, Bleak that people do life's normal chores in Portland: dry cleaning, banking, PO box.

But back to me. In the cold, slender coffin of the family mailbox at the main Portland post office, nestled among the wooden toy catalogs, were three (!) applications to boarding schools that are anywhere but here. My freakish perfect PSAT score apparently has boarding schools deciding, on the same random day, to welcome me to join their leafy fold. (And, really, isn't leafy a step on the road to Ivy?) All that wishing for a different life, and somehow—through osmosis or another permeable technology—it seems to be happening.

So far I'm keeping this good news to myself. Sharing is so banal (Wordly Wise Word!). It's not intellectually mature, but I can't resist pointing out vocabulary from the vexing Wordly Wise Word list. Sometimes I take things too far.

The boat lurches. The air turns aloof, the sun sinks. Dusk is 3:42 this time of year. Something like my heart sinks too. Out in the bay, Portland gets smaller. It's turned into a Shrinky Dinks city.

5

"Candy cane, Charlotte?" I pivot to see Hunky Henry Davensport. He graduated last year vale*dick*torian and then stayed on-island to direct cars and haul lobster traps.

"I'm not biting," I say, shaking my head so fiercely I tilt Eb's stroller.

"Not biting," says Fern, a superb mimic.

If you're a neurotically observant reader you probably pick up on the joke. My family is the cast of *Charlotte's Web*. I am Charlotte, so I started the literary trend. My four-year-old sister is Fern, and my nine-month-old brother is E.B. Our parents are weirdly infatuated with Maine's own E. B. White, among other obsessions. I call my brother "Eb," like Ed. Like a real name.

"Who turns down a candy cane?" Henry asks. "Where's your holiday soul?"

I could confess: My holiday soul is currently consumed with busting out of Lobsterland.

"I'm Jewish," I say. It's half true. I'm half Jew. We don't do Hanukkah or Christmas. We celebrate the Solstice. I'm not making this up.

"With red hair?"

I twirl said hair. Fern twirls too. Eb claps. He's practically hairless.

Henry has a great smile—uncomplicated. "So hold the candy cane upside down. It's a J for Jewish. Or for Jolly."

"Or jackhole," I say, not really meaning he's a jack-hole. Meaning the whole state of Maine is jacked.

He hooks the J onto the V of my shirt, looks right at me, a beat longer than I expect. "I figure this is my chance. Next time I see you, Noah will be lashed to your side, as always."

Not always, apparently. I keep the cane tucked in my cleavage and bounce the stroller downstairs for the rest of the ride. Here's the hierarchy of the three-level vessel, from the top on down: Tourists climb two flights to the outdoor deck for the complete (and completely frozen) open-air view; townies climb one flight to the enclosed deck and peer out the portholes; islanders go down to steerage with the cars. There is absolutely no scenery, but we're the first to get our arctic asses off the boat.

Eb nods off. I draw the fleece blanket over his cheeks. He sticks to my fingers when I pull away. Though I'm desperate to bolt Bleak, I don't like the thought of flee-ing the sibs—or abruptly absent Noah. Fern separates a bag of pretzels into categories: cracked and whole.

"The ones with salt dwell together," she says. She is a sea sponge about vocab. She is four going on sixteen. I am sixteen going on something.

Seeing Fern divide and conquer makes me flicker on Maris, also known as Mom, separating her many med-ications. Is she cracked or whole? The meds are a new accessory for Maris, a recent acquisition following her little incident last month. Right before Thanksgiving she collapsed in the courtroom—in the middle of arguing a malpractice suit, no less. Dad said, "If I knew cooking a free-range bird was going to make you crazy, I wouldn't have asked." She spent Turkey Day—and the two weeks after that—in Casco Hills, a blandly named place for the insane. Or, in her case, the insanely anxious.

I scan my memory of this morning but can't picture Maris packing the pill case in with her briefs—legal, not Hanes. (Don't ask how my mind got there because I live inside myself, and I can't keep up.) Which means it's probable that Maris left her psychopharmaceuticals sitting right out on the kitchen counter. I suck in my lips.

"What? What?" asks Fern.

"Nothing," I say, sliding down the steel-gray wall, a moving target.

Actually, it *is* something. A potentially catastrophic (dogastrophic?) mistake. Our not-so-standard poodle—named Gussy, another strand in Charlotte's convoluted web—likes to stand on her hind legs and chomp through all manner of items: gefilte fish, glitter Band-Aids, telephone receiver (seriously), and her inexplicable favorite, tampons. Wonder if pill cases are poodleproof?

Mental bookmark: Hide anything personal, such as condoms. Imagine the poodle holding a ribbon of

8

Trojans, her head cocked (ha!) to one side? My sextra-curricular activities are, so far, theoretical.

With one hand steadying Eb's stroller, I perch on the bumper of a pickup truck. Fern roosts in my lap, further squashing my ass into the freezing metal. I imagine I'm sitting on a spongy airline seat soaring skyward on Delta Connection flight 754 to Boston, to civilization, to the get-away land of boarding schools, instead of chugging out into the abyss of the bay with diesel fumes for company.

Then I feel it coming. My toes grip the deck, the ball of my foot rocks forward, my heel flicks up. Just like that my left leg, always the left, oscillates at a thousand miles per hour. It's a perfectly twisted tic, if you think about it—a leg that spazzes in place, never going anywhere.

Fern lobs her foot forward, trying to keep time with mine. She can't; nobody can.

"When my leg goes nuts, you stay still," I say to her.

"I like nuts," she says.

I put my hand on her denim knee, feel it jig. She closes her eyes. Her lashes, the world's longest, fan out in a smile. The candy cane, still lodged in my chest, doesn't crack, at least not audibly.

We're trapped in no-man's-water. That's the thing that sucks about a ferry. No matter how much you want to get home, or away from home, it's always the same damn seventeen minutes across.

One (b)

Boom-boom-boom, we are the first three Bleakers off the boat. Up the gentle hill we tramp, the wobbly-wheeled stroller clacking away. The sidewalks have a thick coat of white rock salt frosting. We're walking on a coconut cake.

Here's what you need to know about living on Bleak in seventy-one words or less: If you're not too pathetic, you can walk the circumference in an hour. There are five hundred residents, but the population swells to more than twenty-five hundred in July when the summer swells arrive. There is one school, kindergarten through fifth grade. Then, unless you're unlucky enough to be homeschooled (poor Hannah), you become a ferry slave and head to Portland for a real education. If you can call it that.

I consider running into our itsy grocer, Cadman's—the milk is low—then reconsider. Seems smarter to get our ass(es) home to make sure Mom took her meds and the dog did not.

Our shingle cottage is an eleven-minute walk uphill and to the left—nine minutes if we cut through surly Dr. Cole's yard. Which we do today, possible poodle tragedy and all.

"Move along, move along," Dr. Cole yells from the front door. He stands there at all hours just waiting to be angry.

"Family emergency!" I say, racing.

"Another one?" he asks, not softening his voice. I'm already off his property. Fern lags, but just for a second.

Then our house comes into view at the peak of the pea-gravel road, its steeply pitched roof poking up amid the pines.

Gussy greets us at the moody-blue door with the long plastic pill case dangling from her mouth like a Marlboro Light. M, T, W, TH, F, S, S. . . . I pry the pill case out of Gussy's mouth—licked clean. The poodle has taken an entire week's worth of Mom's pretty new pills. "Shit . . . ake! Holy shiitake!" This is how I pretend I don't have a toxic mouth when I'm with the siblets.

My first thought (not nice, but true): A Labrador would know better than our uniquely unsmart poodle. The Lab, specifically black Lab, is the state dog of

Maine. God forbid my family be like anyone else. They have to pick a fifty-pound poofball that, with a few snips, could pass for topiary. A poodle, especially a simpleton poodle, would not have been my choice, but now I'm stuck loving her.

I sit the sibs at the kitchen table with a bowl of Kashi between them and plug in our only TV on the wooden counter. Fern throws cereal at the TV. Sometimes she is just four. I'll sweep later.

Gussy's tail quivers, and she madly paws the pumpkin pine floor.

"What's Gussy playing?" Fern asks.

"Gussy games."

"Play with her here, where I am," Fern says.

"No, you're there, I'm here."

She mimics, "I'm here, you're there."

I crouch to face Gus and hold her fuzzy snout. Her eyes are a little squinty; her breath, hideous. It was two weeks ago today that Maris, fresh from her unscheduled stay at Casco Hills, came home with a kaleidoscopic collection of pills. Maris is newly returned to work ("to the law," as she says), and it doesn't seem smart to interrupt her legal-eagle day to ask for a briefing on her meds du jour.

I recover her red-leather notebook in the drawer by the phone. Under *P* (Prescriptions, psychiatric) I find what

I need: Klonopin (panic); Luvox (when feeling OCD); Prozac (daily—absolutely no Absolut); Xanax (for flying).

So many medications for one rather small mother.

While the littles zone out, I snatch the National Animal Poison Control magnet from the fridge and bring the could-be-stoned poodle to my side. Gussy exhales. She's heavy. I've dialed the canine 911 with Gus before—also known as the potentially lethal chocolate fondue incident.

Her black coat makes me think: She's always dressed for a funeral.

The dim-sounding vet tech on the other end of the line tells me what I already know: Spoon-feed the poodle hydrogen peroxide and wait a minute for her to vomit. I grab the peroxide from the bathroom, where Dad uses it as mouthwash (more biodegradable than Scope, apparently). Tick. It's a long minute.

Gussy lopes to the lone rug in the living room and finds her footing, then opens her mouth too wide. The terrible ripple starts in her haunches, but nothing comes up. A few false starts, then she gives a huge heave on the rug. Always on the rug.

"Why is Gussy so loud?" Fern asks over the din of the local news. We don't have cable anymore. Dad turned his back on CNN because of what he calls ecologically insensitive coverage.

"Still playing," I yell. I hope I don't sound mad.

"I'm here, you're there," Fern shouts back.

"You're there. I'm here."

Success! The sweet smell of success. In the mucky pile of detritus I count light yellow (7), faint blue (7), pink (7), and mauve (1). All so pale, these pills. I wet a dish towel and clean up the mess. A very small mess, actually, given the big mess my heart would have been in if Gus had OD'd.

She leans into me. Canine gratitude.

Gussy sits regally on her nubby bed, her long, dark paws crossed. Nefertiti back from the near-departed. Then it hits me: My feet are dead. I unbuckle my too-tall shoes and place them on the stairs, heels together, toes pointed out like they're on display, like they're just waiting to be picked up by a leggy girl who is not me, who doesn't need the extra three inches to heighten her plummeting confidence.

With one sock on top of the other to hold my shakes in place, I dial Noah at his dad's house. The phone rings helplessly; no answering machine or cell phone for him (ditto me). Both of our fathers are oddballs that way, not wanting technology to intrude on our Bleak lives.

I hang on, open the cupboard looking for some collection of ingredients to jump out. I'll make a dip. Down comes the rice-wine vinegar, the soy, the sesame, the red pepper flakes. Lots of them. The longer I hold on, the more heat I shake in.

After, say, a hundred rings, there's officially no answer.

I'm thinking that boy should be home now, when another "boy" wanders in. "Hell. O," he says, snapping his ungloved fingers to some imaginary jazz beat. That would be Simon, aka Dad. I smile back wordlessly, the way Eb smiles at me.

There are times it is inconceivable (ha!) the geezer guy with the sketchy beard, the maniac hair, and the bagged-out flannel shirt is related to me. He could be the Unabomber, but not a father figure.

"This always here?" he asks, pointing to a little yellow lamp that has lived on the kitchen counter forever. I nod. "Well, let's save a few kilowatts, shall we?" He clicks the thing off, not even noticing the TV is plugged in, no doubt sucking power by the second.

That's our Simon. He always looks lost, like he walked into the wrong house and has to ask directions. He'd rather be at the office doing his indefinable geek-job or writing letters of protest: alpha-particle radiation (con); sustainable forestry (pro); genetically engineered crops (con). When he is here, he and his laptop are engaged in meaningful online Scrabble matches. They are quite the happy couple.

Fifteen-point word: *Eccentric.*

Five more days and I hope I'll have my own nine-point word for him: *Stranger*. I'll be on the boat to gone.

The phone brrrings. I lunge for the receiver, figuring Noah is finally on-island.

"Hey, you." I am going for blasé. I dip into the dip. It's got kick.

"Simon?" says an unfamiliar female voice. I shut up. My tongue sizzles. "It's crashing down around us," she says, sounding 360 degrees of crazy. "Boom! Hear that? Boom! Can you hear it? It's taken twenty-six years, but it's crashing down."

"Hold your crash." I give Dad the cordless and a shrug. I pant. The dip has rubbed every taste bud on my tongue the wrong way.

"Well," he says after a deep-breath beat. He stares at an invisible spot on the floor. I noiselessly offer up the dip—let him burn a little. "I need some privacy," he says, waving me off. Fine, be private, be rude. It's not like he's Mr. Loquacious (Wordly Wise Word!). He tucks the phone under his chin and makes a U-turn back to the nine-degree weather with his secret caller. "What are the odds," he says into the receiver, receding out of view.

What are the odds he's odd? So extremely high.

"Will you draw?" Fern asks. Eb has fallen asleep on the chintz love seat.

"I've got lots of homework," I say, practicing a lie. I need to leave the kitchen, ditch the dip, start to fill in the blank lines of those fugging apps. "Fug" being the term hottie Mr. (AP Lit) Trice uses as a fuck-substitute in the grand tradition of authors Steinbeck (John) and Mailer (Norman) who had to self-censor back in the day. But Mr. Trice isn't a meticulous researcher. If he was, he'd know that fug also means a musty, stuffy atmosphere; claustrophobic, like a certain island. To me, fug means the whole fucking fog of Bleak.

I get as far as the refrigerator, where I arrange the plastic alphabet letters into my dream: *e-x-i-t*. All four letters are emergency orange. What are the odds?

I wish it were Friday, that my apps were safely Fed-Exed, and that I was on to my new life as a chic fish (lobster?) in a fabulous, nonsaltwater pond. I picture my exiting self crossing the yard, the bay, the state line.

A clump of ice slip-slides down the roof. Thud.

One (c)

Dad is still circling the front yard on the phone, talking in circles, no doubt, to the fanatical-sounding friend of a lifetime ago. I do what I always do when he moseys home—as if today was a normal day. As if I didn't have my off-island escape strategy special-delivered to me hours ago. As if Mom's multisyllabic pills weren't just ingested by the poodle (could she be depressed too?). As if Dad weren't Dad.

I head to the dollhouse hominess of my room, where the walls meet the rafters in what was formerly the attic. I step into my color—ceilings, walls, window trim. I repainted this room last month. It's possible I'm obsessed with color, among other things. I tried ten different blues—carrying little sample cups of each color over on Hunky Henry's ferry—before finding my true hue. Benjamin Moore 2063: Cumulus Cotton.

From up here, from out the little dormer windows, it's a land of sharp roofs and bare branches. I wish it would snow. Snow is the great Liquid Paper. It obliterates mistakes, blurs edges. In snow I can pretend the landscape is fresh and unfamiliar, instead of knowing every slip and curve of the coast.

Breathe. I pinch out my contacts and put on my chunky black frames—the better to read with. Out from under the bed comes the stash of magazines. How scary is it that I talk to myself in that hyper-fem maggie voice? "Are you a beauty virgin? Six pretty ways to lose it!" I see the deviously simple pictures and think: How now? How hard can it be to be a genuine genius in love? Or, to the point tonight, do your own bikini wax?

The apps can wait. And, anyway, mastering fuzz patrol seems an essential prep-school skill. I'm prepping for the prep. I'm warming up.

Literally. I heat the wax pack under H_2O in the old cast-iron tub. It takes forever for the hot water to make it up two flights, but when it arrives, it scorches.

I do a test patch where my fish-belly-white inner thigh meets the edge of my crotch and yank. Yowza.

A little truth in beauty, people!

I'm saved from further waxing by—you'd think I'd say by the bell, but we don't have a doorbell. I'm saved by the slam of the storm door.

Oh, Susannah, my vocab-challenged bestish friend, clomps up the attic stairs to my blue shelter. When she was six, Susannah fell on these steep pine stairs and split her head open. Now every time she goes up or down—probably six-thousand times in the last ten years—I count to make sure she doesn't miss a step. There are sixteen, by the way.

"Noah is brilliant," she says, dumping her book bag on my bed. Her hair is a million different people—choppy bangs and feather layers—with enough plastic clips to outfit an entire gymnastics team. Still, she's pretty. Gorgeous.

"I could help you with vocab," I say. "He's not the only brilliant one."

I'm holding the gauze strip with a circle of pubes stuck to it, which pretty much belies said brilliance.

"You're *too* smart. At least you think you are," she says, reaching over and pinching the gauze with her thumb and finger and pursing her lips. "Nasty."

She opens the window and tosses the gauze. It flutters above Dad's head, still bobbing to his clandestine conversation. She misses.

"Litter girl," I say. I would say more if she hadn't been monopolizing my boyfriend in the dwindling days before I make the *e-x-i-t* to boarding school. Not that she—or he—could guess this is on my mind. I gnaw my lip.

Chalk it up to another worthless habit—not the lip, but being mad at people about things they can't possibly know.

"Ch-ch-ch-change-changing the subject," she sings,

her head pecking forward. Now she looks stupid, and I'm happier. "What do you have for Friday night?" She doesn't wait for an answer. She's stuck on the tell part of show-and-tell. "My dress is startling—that's an easy SAT word. I got that one right today." Whoop-de-fug. "It's strong pink at the top then it fades—shush!—into a pale, pale pink at the bottom. I want to win so bad."

Lobster Goddess is what she's after—in addition, I'm guessing, to Noah. The goddess will be crowned (clawed?) at Friday's Solstice Festival in the boathouse. It's an annual ritual, one of those traditions people "from away" read about in winter issues of *Down East* and find so utterly charming. We know better. We know it's stifling. There is no air in the boathouse, for one thing.

"Badly. You want to win badly." I can't help myself.

"No, I want to win bad." Susannah grabs Leo, my lumpy stuffed lobster, and holds it over her head. An ad hoc crown.

We reblonded her hair in my scalding tub two weeks ago. Against the faded red of old Leo she looks a little brassy. Out of all the fake-hair hanks in the Portland CVS, we picked Starfish Dark Blonde. Why not have color karma on her goddess side? See what I mean about the color obsession?

"Who will be your king?" I ask, taking Leo. Clutching him, really.

"There is no king." She's a literal girl.

"Your date, blondie. Who is your date?"

"A surprise." Hunky Henry, perhaps?

I yank out the vintage dress (yay for eBay) I bought for Friday night. Assuming a small thing: that Noah doesn't dropkick me when I tell him about boarding school. We've gone to every Solstice dance together since we were twelve. This year he's going vintage too: a narrow-lapel suit. Think early John Lennon.

I hold up the dress: super simple, navy blue, with a billion little buttons up the back. I divert on Noah's long fingers fingering those many, many little buttons.

"Oh. Retro. Like Jackie O," Susannah says. I should let this go. But I'm not a big person—literally, certainly, or in any other way.

"No. Retro like Audrey," I say. "Like *Breakfast at Tiffany's*. The movie or, better yet, the book. Not like that lame Deep Blue Something song you hum when your dad plays lite rock. Don't deny it."

Susannah's face flushes, and her hair tumbles down from its impromptu updo. "Must be nice to always know absolutely every useless thing."

"There are things I don't know." We teeter on the edge of a fight. Susannah looks down, and I drill my eyes into the top of her head. She has dandruff. As a sign of great maturity, I keep this information to myself. "I don't know why, to take one minuscule case in point, my best friend suddenly invents a pretext to study with my boyfriend," I say.

There's a pause, then Susannah flips me off. She grabs her backpack. "Your dress," she says, pointing at me with a sparkly nail, "is hideous. The ugliest length. Go ahead and wear the highest heels you can find. You will still have piano legs."

I scramble the count of the stairs on her way down—16, 13, 15, 11, 9, 12. . . . I listen for her to stumble, but she doesn't, of course.

Apparently the burning has begun. The edge of my crotch burns, for one thing. In a more public (less pubic) way, I mean I'll scorch bridges before I leave. Burning bridges takes on a whole new meaning when you live on-island. You want to be sure to be standing on the Maineland when the smoke clears.

To cool down, even though it's fugging cold, I get under the covers fully clothed. I consider not talking to anyone whose words aren't close to my own. Or speaking only in Hebrew, which is essentially the same thing. This lasts six minutes.

Noah is home when I try again. When he answers I say, "Susannah is devil spawn." Actually, I don't say that out loud. I say "hey" and agree to meet him at Cadman's in ten minutes.

You'd think I'd be secure enough with Noah to stay in

glasses and garden clogs. As Maris would say, so sue me. I push in the contact lenses and force my sore toes back into the olive stilettos, even though the streets are skiddy.

At the back door, I catch this glimpse of Dad, the spy who has come in from the cold. He sits on the floor of the den reading to the sibs from *The New Republic*. I'll give him that it's a clever liberal maggie. But what can a four-year-old and nine-month-old possibly take in about the state of Israeli health care?

He's changed from his scraggly work clothes to his even-more-scraggly home clothes—holey jeans and a faded Yale tee, circa 1977. It's possible he owns no garment manufactured post-millennium.

Fern jumps up and hands me a drawing she's made. A few lines, a squiggle, and a circle.

"Tell me about it," I say, crouching so that our heads are lined up.

"It's Gussy and our house. And you," she says, pointing to the sphere.

I give her a kiss at the curve of her mouth and whisper, "Thanks."

Odds are I'll miss these moments, these squiggles. I take the orange *e* alphabet magnet from its *e-x-i-t* grouping and slam it into service to hang my portrait front and center on the fridge. There are two pencil dots on my face—I hardly have eyes.

One (d)

On my way to meet Noah, I trudge through frozen grass to get a little traction. Even so, I beat him. I duck into Caddy's to buy a few necessities: milk, bagels, adzuki beans, cranberry granola (for my crunchy siblets), tiny Niçoise olives (imported, natch, for Maris), and Cocoa Puffs and Coca-Cola (for me, my lame act of rebellion).

"You guys go through a lot of cranny granny," Norma the cashier says. She has the distinction of always, but always, smelling flatulent. Hey, I'd rather my family be known for a granola habit than Norma's vaporous claim to fame.

"Hold on," I say to the air. No one is behind me. "One more thing." I grab a folder with a ridiculous cartoon lobster from the school supply shelf. Half price since it's locals-only season. The perfect cover for application materials meant to take me straight out of Lobsterland.

By the time I check out, Noah is under the leaking awning looking pretty cute, ski cap yanked down over his ears, the little hunk of hair I cut for him when we were bored last summer poking out. He can pass for twelve or pass for twenty. I like that he can go either way. Love pretty much every bit of his keratin.

I step on his all-terrain boot with my nonboot, careful not to stab him with my stiletto.

He practices safe making out—looks right, then left, then comes in for the kiss. Such a cautious boy. Officially noted: He pulls back first. My hand gets scratchy in my mitten.

I take the mitty off and fist my way into the pocket of his puffy parka. He carries my eco-friendly canvas bag of groceries. The air is that sshh-quiet that comes before major snow.

Which, for some reason, makes me regress to our playground chant, circa 1992: "This is a game . . ."

He catches on right away. Such a quick boy. "Of concentration . . ."

"No repeats . . ."

"Or hesitations."

"I'll go first."

"You always go first," he says, jabbing me in the shoulder, not hard, but not with love either. But he picks up the tune, "I'll go second."

I start. "The category is"—*clap clap*—"P"—*clap clap*.

"Prozac." *Clap clap.*

"Portland." *Clap clap.*

"Poodle."

"Profound."

"Poe, as in Edgar."

"Pie, as in pecan."

"Prep." Shit. But he doesn't notice.

"PMS."

"Proletariat." I have the last word.

"How's Susannah's vocab coming?" I ask. I turn to look at him and actually slip (as opposed to Freudian) on a patch of black ice. He catches my elbow and sets me right.

"Well, it's not what you'd call prodigious. In fact, she thought *prodigious* meant pathetic." He stops. "Are you weird?"

I shake my hat no and kiss him, still shaking. This is how prodigiously pathetic I am.

Noah walks me home the long way, past Key's Lobster Pound and the new awayers who want to open a shipwreck museum. Like that's an original idea on an island.

I inhale the copyrighted smell, half bleach, half brine, of the incoming tide. And I wonder: Do tides get bored doing the same old cha-cha on the same old shore? Do they ever want to quit or die of ennui (Wordly Wise Word!)? Or just transfer out?

The pea-soupy fog follows me home. When I open the door it evaporates, poof. I walk into a kind of Hallmark moment: Eb huddles on Mom's lap—she must have made the 6:15 ferry—listening to her read Longfellow poetry. Fern plays tug-o'-war with Gussy, who looks positively alive. Dad engages in Scrabble sex with his mistress, Lola the laptop. Everyone's got a partner. Everyone but me.

Without actually shifting her gaze, Maris snaps, "Charlotte Alice."

"Present."

"As your note so kindly indicates, the dog ate my medication."

To avoid maternal confrontation, I'd left a Post-it on the fridge half under Fern's drawing: "Gussy crunched pills. Sorry!"

Mom's nose is so deep down in the poetry book, it's like she wants to melt into the page. "I'm glad Gussy is all right," she says, without an overdose of conviction. "But see things, if you will, from my perspective. My refills aren't due until next week. It's not like I can expedite the process of a mail-order medication mill." She catches her breath. "And even if I can, at the least it seems I'll be off for one, two, even three days." She lifts up from Longfellow and looks dead into my eyes.

"Everything's hunky-fucking-dory," she says unpoeti-cally. This is where I get my trucker mouth tendencies. My genetic link to Mom.

"I can help you get your refills together," I say. "I can make some calls or whatever." The groceries are getting heavy. I list to the left. "Can I get you some olives?"

"I'm capable," she says. "It's not that I'm not capable."

"I didn't say that." Hey, I didn't.

"It was a surprise to see your note. I'm not much for surprises right now."

Mental bookmark: Don't be a sharer. It's not like I am falling over myself to share the escape plan, anyway. The parents would see no need to flee. When they ran-domly moved from Manhattan to Maine, taking me without my consent (I was in utero), they bought into that Walden simple-life fantasy. My departure will throw their failure(s) into relief. There's also the little matter of who will care for the littles, but I've worked that out. Fern will be in kindergarten in the fall. And Eb, well, he's a third. He's easy-pleasy.

I scan Dad for a reaction to Mom's pout, but he's so focused on his laptop and his online Scrabble opponent (perhaps Sigrun from Reykjavik again), I can't catch his eye. Actually, he's fuck-us-ed, according to my Israeli

Hebrew teacher with the raspy accent. "Fuck-us," she yells when I drift off during mind-numbing Hebrew school. It's amazing how often one can work *fuck-us* into everyday conversation.

To wrap up the weirdness of Dad's focused/fuck-us-ed Scrabble obsession: He spent all his free time last summer making his own Scrabble dictionary. Like the million Scrabble dictionaries already published have some *über*deficiency. He thinks this is the next big idea, a tiny booklet small enough to fit into a back pocket.

His first entry: *Aahed*, meaning an expression of delight. As in oohed and aahed. But pronounced odd. Of course. A truer meaning for my family.

One (e)

I escape quality family time (cough, cough) by ducking into my snug room under the blue eaves to do more nonexistent homework. I can't remember the last time I had real work to do at home, as opposed to busy work to do between bites of turkey meatloaf (blecch) at lunch. Still, I've got a weighted GPA of 4.45 thanks to honors classes, not to mention that perfect PSAT.

All righty, time to turn on the Clash. Because London is calling. Or at least prep schools are calling. I squoosh down on the duvet with my laptop. My leg jiggles to the tune, which makes the screen bbbounce a bit. The shake is an odd tic of late, but perhaps it will give the essay that certain syncopated *je ne sais quoi.*

Useless knowledge: The chickadee, Maine's state bird, does not fly south in the winter. All its feathered peers haul ass out of town. Like me, the bird with wings is in lockdown.

Anytime I'm any other place—in Brooklyn or Santa Monica or with some Massholes—I run into people who sigh-smile when I concede I'm from an island off the coast of Maine.

They're thinking lighthouses, lobsters, Wyeth. They often add the spectacularly insipid comment "I went to summer camp in Maine."

For the record, going to camp in Maine has nada to do with living here 334 days a year.

For those who are anal about keeping track of such things, here are the days I'm away: five days in Brooklyn every Passover to visit Dad's clan, twelve days at "draahma" camp in "Sarrah-toga," a week in Santa Monica at some point so Mom can strut down memory lane, and the annual good-for-you vacation to, maybe, Vancouver, British Columbia, to see the birthplace of Greenpeace.

Let's just say Greenpeace was the original teen radical group. Dad was rad back when being a revolutionary was cool. There are pictures of him in the upstairs hallway protesting on the deck of an oil tanker, picketing lumber giants that deforest, sitting in at a nuclear reactor—that kind of crap.

My friends who think the seventies were all Ashton Kutcher–cute with feathered hair and Pop Rocks find the image of Dad with an unexploded hand grenade quite the reality spank.

It could be worse. He could be more of a humiliation. Lucia's dad has attended a Renaissance festival in all fifty states.

Breathe. Application essay question number one.
WHAT DO YOU LIKE BEST ABOUT YOURSELF? WHY?

How about a few pages of what I don't like? Starting with the physical (too little in the femur, too large in the boobular). Or the metaphysical (transcending the place I was born and the family I was born into, because I really need to do that as soon as possible). Or the nightmare/daymare of sitting in the deep-dark of my room and being scared—not of the bogeyman (or the lobsterman) but of how much I mislike my parents.

I sit up too fast and bam my head into my beloved eaves.

Instead, let's try short-answer number three.
WE TEACH THE FOLLOWING LANGUAGES: GREEK, SWATI, JAPANESE, LATIN, CHINESE, FRENCH, AND SPANISH. PLEASE INDICATE WHICH OF THESE LANGUAGES YOU SPEAK OR WISH TO STUDY.
Sloppy copy:

D'accord! *I've taken high school French for a year and two months and speak French poorly. I have* beaucoup de *books, however, on living in France and plan one day to live in my own* petit apartment in the seventh arrondissement. *My class average is 100 (out of 100), which probably isn't that high, given the type of student you attract. I'm probably considerably less brilliant than your typical applicant, even though I'm quite the catch in our little Maine pond. The truth is you have to be* très, très stupide *in my school to get less (or is it lower?) than a 95.*

I'm not only fluent in English, but also several unrelated dialects. Maine-speak is a regional vernacular that includes words like wicked *(meaning "very, to a high degree"—as in wicked good), and* from away *(meaning "not originally from Maine"—as in my family).*

In addition, I speak a sprinkling of kinder-Yiddish, a hybrid of German and Yiddish perfected by my father when he doesn't want me to understand what he is saying. Example: His colleague David Avery is a tochus laeker *(ass kisser) who eclipsed and now may fire my father.*

I've also rote-memorized a number of Hebrew prayers, the result of going to worship services the second Friday of the month (Friday Night Live!) at the synagogue down the coast. To be honest—a trait I find important in any language—I don't really know the meaning of these Hebrew words, even though I've spent ten years off and on in Hebrew school, and even though our rabbi is hysterical and has a trailer-trash aura (he grew up in Montgomery, Alabama, which may be one place that is bleaker than Bleak). But back to my language skills. I've mouthed the Hebrew prayers so frequently, they've become quasimeaningful. Shalom!

As a child I made up my own language. Bananas were baseballs, and my friends were always named Polly (Polly one, Polly two, Polly three). My father, a good sport once upon a time, became Penny, and we lived on the island of Prize (before it was somehow taken away) and spoke the language of Pesto.

I realize this is really not *what you need to know about me—especially since I don't remotely speak the language of my family these days. These days, I need a translator. Or at least a flashlight. I need a strong, ideally rechargeable, beam to shine around to see what the hell is happening on this island where it gets dark at 3:42 on a winter's afternoon.*

As for future study, given the rich multi-culti landscape of your school, I imagine I might be motivated to take Japanese. I've always had an interest in origami.

Clearly the essay needs more focused/fuck-us-ed thought.

I've got ninety-two hours to make it better. The keeping of a secret—the omission of key radioactive details like how long Mom will be on crazy meds or whose ear Dad was whispering into, or when/if I will share my boarding school escape scheme—makes me coil.

My left leg quakes like the San Andreas f-f-f-fault.

Useless knowledge: Maine is earthquake country too. Sure, everybody knows that California is going to drop off a sea cliff someday. But there have been nine notable tremors Down East.

It will be my luck that the big one will hit my island instead of, say, their Irvine. Everyone worries about the wrong thing.

From my high room, I notice the house is quiet. It's like I've already left—or, worse (better?), like the family has left me by surprise.

One (f)

I am seduced out of conjugating French verbs in my *bleu* attic by the drifting smell of the woodstove in full blaze downstairs. I imagine the family nucleus gathering at the hearth. Even the frosty are drawn by flames. Even I am not fireproof.

When I come down, the fire is perfect, but no one is paying attention. I grab the last slice of smoked salmon pizza Maris must have picked up from the new flat-bread place in Portland.

"You want to join the game?" Dad asks. He's set up a Scrabble board on the pine trunk.

"Just thirsty." I pop open a can of Coke—chugging the bubbles like they're a prescription, which in a way they are—and turn on the TV, the electronic hearth, still out on the kitchen counter from this afternoon's sidetrack-the-siblets-while-saving-Gus adventure.

On the only channel we actually get reception for, I watch the pathetic host of that *Top Ten Wanted* show who "lost" his son a million years ago. Kidnapped? Okay, that's appalling and all, but won't he ever move on?

It's like Susannah, my formerly best friend: She blames every dismal thing, every single C-plus, on her parents splitting up. That's her story, and she's sticking to it, no matter how many times she's bored herself by starting a sentence: "If my parents were still together. . . ."

She could just decide to tell another story. Why the hell not? Good writers rewrite a line fifty or sixty times, according to Mr. (AP Lit) Trice.

The TV host with the comb-over is droning on about this week's wanted, a search for some Pale Chick who went underground in 1978 for bombing a car or bombing a bar or, less likely, a guitar.

But I forget about the loser who's talking and focus/fuck-us on the person next to Pale Chick. Actually the elbow next to Pale Chick. Before I completely process the image, my leg begins its quake-and-shake. The tremble jams my knee into the counter. Coke sloshes out of the can.

I want to click enlarge, enlarge to be sure. But the hard knock of the leg tells me that, yeah, I know the elbow. Well, not the elbow so much as the shirt.

It is Dad's flannel shirt, the very one he was wearing as of several hours ago. The flannel shirt from Beans.

Small digression to touristas and former campers: No one says L. L. Bean. No. One. You've got to drop the double *L* and add an *S*. As in garbanzos. Let's practice: Beans.

I turn back and see a glimpse of a tear on the shirt-sleeve—or could it be a patch caught sideways? He's had that plaid shirt since grad school, and it's got a heart-shaped (cringe!) denim patch he maniacally sews up anytime one of the precious little stitches comes loose.

That's some metaphor: wearing his heart on his sleeve.

I yank the plug out of the counter. It sparks.

"Need to ground that outlet—it's an energy sap," Dad says from the safe shelter of his Scrabble board. "Ready to join in?" If he was listening, he doesn't let on.

"Be on my team," says Fern. She turns the smooth letter tiles over and over, not building words so much as building a slippery steeple.

Sometimes the family doesn't seem substantially weirder than others on-island. They don't call us Maini-acs for nothing. Mom reads a French fashion maggie, unaware of sparks, literal or otherwise. Eb drinks water from a sippy cup, his eyes looking past me. Gussy chews on a stuffed moose.

What would be normal in a normal family—say, hmm, Noah's? What if I put *my* heart on *my* sleeve and say to Dad, "Whoa, isn't that your favorite flannel shirt on that fugitive dude?" Maybe not the dude part because Noah's mom is a linguistic purist who believes surfer slang leads—eventually—to crack use. But still. In this house, we go mute when the going gets tough. Odd/aahed for a bunch of wordies.

"I'm not done watching," I say. I carefully reinsert the prongs into the plug for a zing-free connection. When the TV flickers back on, there's a commercial for luncheon meat. My sudden burning hunger isn't for bologna. I want to rewind to the video that's already evaporated into thin satellite air. Did they say they were looking just for Pale Chick or did she have cohorts-at-large? What was her crime, with or without Dad lending a hand, or elbow? Was anyone hurt? Killed? Once again, I overjumped the story. As Mr. (AP Lit) Trice says: linear progression—not my strength.

I rewind to all the times I told Dad that dressing like a bum was criminal.

I rewind to his eccentricities. He (1) never joins us when we visit California—"I don't need to be reminded how your mother married beneath her"—(2) heads outside to take mysterious phone calls in the subarctic, and (3) won't drink.

This suddenly seems huge, his not wanting to be condemned by a cocktail. We all know how alcohol can loosen the tongue. After just one (strongish) Tequila Sunrise, Zach Forest, he of the forest of zits, told me about his wet dreams. All together now: ew.

"Hey, Dad, can I pour you a glass of wine?" I say, suddenly a DA gathering evidence. If he imbibes, then he has nothing to hide.

"Very funny. You can bring me some carrot juice."

So there you go. One day his teeth will be orange.

What's a high-scoring word for busting loose? *Vamoose?* Whatever it is, that's what I want to do.

One (g)

Dad doesn't believe in anything as conformist as regular bedtime. It's near ten before he finally tucks the siblets in and I am free to go in search of the shirt off his back.

As soon as I hear him start *Blueberries for Sal* (kuplink-kuplank-kuplunk), I paw through the wicker hamper on my parents' hooked rug, also from Beans. The rug has concentric circles of rose and khaki. It's reversible. Also lifeless. That's where Beans falls flat. Useful is one thing, chic quite another.

My hands are on the wet side from washing my face with ginger-peach exfoliator (please let it be a break-out-free week) so I don't recognize the soft flannel at first. It's there, of course, heart intact.

The plaid is so faded, it's hard to imagine it has had a checkered (ha!) past. Such an innocent little lump of flannel. It smells faintly sweet, unlike many of Dad's clothes, which don't encounter detergent, biodegradable or not, often enough for my nose.

Lightbulb: I will sleep in this shirt. I will pull him over my shoulders, button his history over my camisole. I will get under his skin. I carefully thread my hands through the sleeves so as not to disturb the heart.

No longer coked on Coke, I walk downstairs for a drink of water. For a drink of water and a reaction, let's face it. Waltz right past Maris, who is listening to a CD of thundering rainstorms. The un-music is supposed to be soothing.

"Can I get you anything?" I stand right in front of her, arms akimbo.

Her eyes are incurious. Conceivably, she's still thick on this morning's medication. "There isn't a thing I need."

I pour myself not one glass of water, but two. I'm not entirely sure why this seems defiant, but it does. "Your loss," I say, taking both glasses upstairs.

The two glasses, one full, one now empty, sit on my desk to watch over me while I snuzzle into my blue—cerulean, technically—duvet. I have water on the brain—phony thunderstorms, running faucets, the placid Casco Bay. My mind swims farther, deeper, weirder.

I plunge ahead six years and imagine I'm with Noah. Whoops, someone who looks like Noah but is not him.

We are at the Sorbonne. I don't know what people study at the Sorbonne, but I excel at most stuff, save for Organic Chem—I reflexively hate all things organic, of course. Not-Noah and I have a small, high-ceilinged apartment with honey-colored walls and big pine shutters that fling open to the sun.

No flashlight needed here.

The windows look out over the Seine, which doesn't have the lap-crash sound effects of the Atlantic, but, hey, it's water. There's a dog too, though not a poodle—sorry, Gussy. (Useless knowledge: Poodles are actually German, not French. Still, I'd rather a dog I don't have to explain. I'd rather a dog that wasn't so fugging fancy.) I'd throw together amazing meals and serve them on mismatched but beautiful old china I'd pick up for a song (a *chanson*!) at a flea market. We'd have mucho (*beaucoup*!) life-changing sex.

I half wonder how this relates to my prep-school dream. I half consider keeping my dreams in sequence, but I like this one, like the food and the sex. Not-Noah and I have a house full of golden light and sweet-smelling clothes. And music, normal, tuneful music, nothing that could remotely be considered weather. Please, let's keep weather out of it altogether.

TUESDAY

Two (a)

I wake up with Dad's radical plaid shirt wound and wrapped over my whole torso, clinging limpetlike.

I jump out of bed to untangle myself. And want to jump back in. Today's expected high: seven degrees.

Instead I make myself a deal. I will bring the warm-and-fuzzy contraband to school, but I will also stay downstairs after dinner. No fleeing to my room or to my Noah. I will have a conversation with the family or at least the Maris, the one most likely to give and take. Especially if I pour her some Pinot.

The trick is to not overobsess until then.

Coincidentally, I'm an overachiever when it comes to avoidance.

After the usual morning sacraments—munch granola, catch ferry, kiss Noah, drop tots at Small World—I land, on time, in first period. I speed through hottie Mr. Trice's *Black Boy* test. As long as I sling *fuck-fuck-fuck* throughout my answers, he'll think I've internalized the great Richard Wright's oeuvre.

Today I wear tweedy pumps with pointy toes, and I kick them off to sit cross-legged in the When . . . You . . . Are . . . Finished . . . corner scanning, scouring, searching, pursuing, panning (enough!) the big red *Synonym Finder* to find the right word for *independent*.

I need to persuade Mr. Trice that it's not necessary to check with my Bleak parents before writing the b.s. (nice irony—boarding school *and* bullshit) recommendations.

Not to sound narcissistic, but I figure I'll get in. The admission material came right out and said, "We invite you to be part of next year's junior class." Whether I'll fit in is a different story. The brochures show kids with crested shirts and Crest smiles. I wonder if my skin will even be allowed to break out. If it does, I'll probably be immediately relegated to the unsmilers, the unphotographed.

Okay, back to the sunny side before I get into an insecurity spiral like a certain maternal figure.

Luckily, I'm the one who stops by the post office, so when the b.s. news comes, I will have it to myself (for a while, anyway—why share until absolutely required?).

Doubly luckily, Maris and Simon never dig around in my room, making them unlikely to happen across any applications in progress. They claim they're respecting my personal liberty. Really, they just don't care.

I am not interesting enough. It's as simple, and as twisted, as that. I have tried to bait them by leaving a condom packet, shiny like a peppermint patty, out on my bed. But curiosity stops at the bottom of the stairs.

Okay, less sunny: Someone thought it would be a good idea to paint the cinder-block walls in Mr. Trice's room a dreary lavender. The color of a bruise, like we're all the walking wounded. Don't these people have any, *any* appreciation for the power of color?

And even gloomier, Bayside's problems extend beyond the palette.

There's the little fact that forty-two percent of our class won't go to a four-year college. Perfectly brainy kids make the decision to not go to any college at all, not even a bumblefuck place like KKK (that's Koastal Kommunity Kollege). I don't get it. If they don't leave for school, they tend not to leave, period. They become lifers. Even Hunky Henry.

Obviously, home is where my heart is, uh, not. Reason number forty-two for wanting to propel myself to prep school.

In order of preference: Lawrenceville (376 miles away); Hotchkiss (248 miles away); and Phillips Andover (109 miles away).

The last thigh-tight-jeans girl files out of Mr. Trice's lavender-bruised room, and I feel that annoying hot cheek-flush set in as I wait for Mr. T. to turn around and notice I've stayed behind.

Okay. 1, 2, 3, 4, 5, 6, 7, 8, 9, 10, 11, 12, 13, 14 . . . (If he doesn't turn around by 45, I'll speak up. Useless knowledge: 45 is a magic number in air safety. If a plane is going to crash, odds are it's in the first 45 seconds. Get to 46, and breathe easy.) . . . 32, 33, 34, 35, 36, 37.

He pivots on his Birkie sandal and says, "Charlotte, what's on that formidable mind of yours?"

I could say I worry that my nut-job father is a fugitive. Or that my mother is an actual nut. Or that my dog might OD for good. Or that my siblets will grow up thinking Bleak life really is serene (as opposed to suffocating). But why share?

"I have a favor to ask, Mr. Trice." I finger the sea glass necklace Fern made me, looking for the little good-luck groove.

"Call me Lars."

I try to keep from cocking my head like a dog. Is he flirting? Ew. I'm so sure his school bio says Larry. Lars sounds pompous. Plus, I flash on the *Little Polar Bear* book that Eb adores. I'm quite sure the protagonist polar is Lars.

"I was hoping you'd write me a recommendation to Lawrenceville and a few other lesser schools," I say, trying for a tone of insouciance (Wordly Wise Word!). I hand over the trying-hard-to-be-cheerful lobster folder

I picked up to organize/hide the school apps. "I know you went there—Lawrenceville, I mean. And it would mean a lot to me."

"It would be a loss for our academic community if you left," he says, looking all old. I wonder if his hair is dirty under his hat with earflaps. "Your scores are essential to the sophomore class." He means I am a feather in his woodsman cap.

"Well, I love this place (ha), love your class (quasi ha), and I would miss the island (moo ha ha), but I think it's time to get a little more autonomous." *Merci, Synonym Finder.*

Logically: "And your family? How will they thrive without their Charlotte?"

"They encourage me to think for myself," I say, not exactly answering his question. Still, this nub of honesty snags in my throat. I cough.

"I'd be honored," he says, tugging on my ponytail. Is he petting me? Maybe he's mocking me, but I don't think so. Even though there are those who think Mr. Trice is once, twice, thrice times a hottie, he doesn't have much charm.

Maybe this is what happens at prep school. You enter a furtive parallel universe where "teacher's pet" takes on a literal meaning.

— — —

At this point, it would make perfect sense to find Noah at lunch (taco salad!) and casually bring up the whole did-I-mention-I-was-exploring-schools conversation. Instead I hide out in the library. Sorry, the media center. Painted, for the record, slate blue, another shade in the contusion collection. I've gone from the peaceful private blue of my attic to a bruise to a contusion. I've lost control of my color wheel.

I decide to look for a recipe for dinner inspiration on Epicurious (a curiously great site, indeed), but there's some Freudian typing going on. My fingers jig like my leg and, *voilà*, I type Dad's name into Dogpile's search engine. Score:

- the press release announcing his appointment to senior VP of dipshit software (last year),
- a donation to the Sierra Club (whoop-de-fug),
- an entry in *The Rad Handbook: A Who's Who in Radical History* listing him as both Simon Wise and Si Wiseman (Dad with an alias!),
- a message he sent to Down East Kayakers praising the new Scamper model (which he splurged on while Maris was up a creek in the psych ward),
- eleven letters he wrote to Bush 41 about acid rain, urbanization, biogenetic pollution, and ozone depletion. Twenty-seven letters to Bush

43 on all of the above, plus environmental racism (ironic how landfills turn up near public housing).

I use Mom's Amex (card number and expiration date memorized!) to order *The Rad Handbook* off Amazon. The book will be here in seven business days—too late to be useful for my b.s. applications. Still, I want to know about Simon/Si. There's no statute of limitations for knowing the truth, especially if it's dirty, about one's bona fide father.

For the hell of it, I pull the fugitive shirt out of my backpack, where it's been lying in wait all morning. The puddle of flannel sits between my knees. It balls itself up, kittenlike. I hate cats, so make that puppylike.

I click on over to the Beans site. It's possible every man who has a Che Guevara poster owns a shirt like Dad's. It's possible Beans still sells that tacky tattersall.

Well, guess what? No sign of said plaid on the Beans site (even in the dreaded hunting section). Wardrobe incrimination!

I'm late to *Français*. Are all French teachers on crack?

Madame Lamb lectures us about not passing up sex if we have the opportunity. My translation skills aren't textbook, but still. Ew.

Just as I'm thinking the day will never end, *voilà*! the bell brrrings, and I do the mad dash across to the post office (junk mail), then down the cobblestones to pick up the siblets.

Standing in the doorway of Small World, where I used to be the star toddler, I get a little pang that some nanny type will be taking over my afternoon duty next year.

Fern straightens her shoulders into ballet posture and says *au revoir* to a circle of well-scrubbed girls. "Did you hear my French?" she asks me.

"Flawless," I say, giving her a *petite* kiss at the top of her French braid.

I wonder if next year's nanny will speak *Français*. I can always send Fern tapes from my boarding school's no-doubt-fabulous language lab.

Eb throws his arms around Berjan, my old preschool teacher, who scoops him up like a puppy and sets him in our open stroller, ready to roll.

Outside, we laugh and slide so fast that we leave our voices trailing behind, vanishing into the shivery ether.

This time, Noah is already on the ferry.

This time I am wearing the lower-heeled pumps, and guess what? We still almost miss the boat.

Which goes to show: Function doesn't trump fashion. So ha.

Two (b)

On the mid-deck, I nuzzle into Noah, one ear pressed to his chest, the other catching the wind. Fern stands on the back of Eb's stroller, and Noah rocks them to and fro with his free hand. The ride is too short for a valid nap, but I take a few minutes of drowsy solace leaning into Noah's puffy parka. In my semidream state I forget I'm leaving him behind.

Then boom-boom-boom, the four of us are on-island. Noah takes my hand and we each use our outer mitties to guide the stroller, like we're one giant person. We head to Caddy's to pick up dinner stuff.

Mom's theory: If you want real food, make it yourself. Her corollary: Time is a precious resource, and it shouldn't be wasted at the kitchen sink. This gets her out of dish duty and also serves as her excuse to use the taboo (i.e., landfill-sustaining) paper plates.

Six nights out of seven, I do the cooking. Tonight's menu is couscous with garbanzos, pine nuts, and feta.

Noah sets off to the freezer case to get the siblets Popsicles. Icy treats don't melt as fast in December as they do in July. That's one good thing about winter.

While I wait to pay, Fern offers a bite of her grape pop to Chloe, who has appeared from somewhere. Chloe is three years older than Fern and homeschooled. Enough said. Fern looks at me for permission, and I nod. We do nonverbal well: Yes, Chloe can come over. Even though Chloe is a biter, it's nice to have a friend.

Now we are five. Up the hill we chug, Noah pushing Eb, Fern and Chloe holding pinkies, me swinging the groceries.

Gussy sits at the storm door thumping her tail in greeting, no psycho meds in sight. Yay.

It's a bright picture. Plus, very literally on the bright side, the kitchen glitters with that golden, nearly orange light that comes with the sunset. We all look ridiculously happy and tan.

Chloe gives Gussy a bite, a gentle one, on the back, like she's having a good time. The glacial day forgotten, I pretend I am cooking a perfectly magnificent meal in Provence.

I tuck Eb in for a quickie nap, kiss his sticky cheek, and head back to the kitchen to toast the pine nuts in the iron skillet.

Noah skims the newspaper. The *New York Times*, specifically, part of Maris's island denial. She has been here sixteen years and still insists on her urbanities. They seem to me *sub*urban. Not as in suburbia (a fate worse than Maine), but as in *sub-par* urban. As in someone who insists on home delivery of the *Times* and insists on making quarterly pilgrimages to Marco in Manhattan to keep her highlights high.

Fish out of water much?

At the kitchen table, the girls are playing office.

"Ring-ring-ring," Fern says. She picks up a banana. "Phone call for Charlotte." She walks over and hands me the banana-receiver.

"I'm making dinner. Take a message, please."

"It's crucial," she says, dress-rehearsing her grown-up vocab. "It's Daddy."

Damned if I don't pick up the Chiquita and say, "Who the hell is Si? Who are you? Who is that girl? And . . . who do you think you are to never change your socks?"

How tightly wound must I be if an innocent source of potassium sets me off?

I throw the banana across the counter—hot potato, hot potassium, hot topic—and force a laugh out of my tight throat.

The girls aren't listening anyway. Fern gives Chloe an

assignment. She's moved on to her next profession—teacher. "Spell toasterrain," Fern says. "Spell divviedom." She's got nothing on the homeschooler.

Noah peels the Chiquita and stuffs half of it in his mouth. I can't tell if he heard me and is letting it go or is coincidentally hungry.

"Can you give the skillet a shake so the nuts won't scorch?" I ask. "Be back in three."

He nods; his hair swings yes.

Destination: Dad's office, the recipient of another one of my recent redecorating projects. I camouflaged the banged-up paneling by painting it the prettiest, mistiest gray. Gray now seems a metaphorical choice—vague and blurry.

Gussy trots along after me, then lies on the old jute rug. I half pet her with my foot. The could-be-a-topiary poodle flips over and splays her hind legs. Nothing for her to hide whatsoever.

Okay, this is the plan I made up just this minute: to go through the enormous stack of pictures Dad keeps in a wooden box, not really big enough to be called a trunk.

I tip the lid and catch a hint of something sweet—cedar? weed? baby powder? Likely all of the above. I trace my finger over the smooth rim, imagine him opening the box when he was sixteen or twenty-six or forty-two and slipping memories inside.

Right on top I see that queer wedding picture: Dad whispering to Mom, with the world's most cliché fountain in the background. Not just one copy of the photo but a stockpile. Actually, twenty-three. I count.

For whatever reason, Maris loves this shot. Once, when I asked what was up with the geyser, she answered defensively, "Not everything is ironic, Charlotte."

Since when?

"What I remember most from that day," she went on, "is Simon whispering 'I love you' two thousand times and, fountain or no, seeing his mouth at my ear makes me smile." And me nauseated.

At the bottom of the not-trunk, my hands land on a blue envelope, thin as smoke, with pictures inside. I hesitate. What if the pictures are nothing, what if they're something? What if the envelope disintegrates in my fingers?

Well, it doesn't. I slip out the slender pile of images and quickly slide the photos past each other. Where is Maris?

First weird shot: a dorkish sunset captured in intervals with a topless girl (ew) in the far background. Is she the Pale Chick from TV trying to get a tan?

Second: a faded image of Dad standing on a chair audaciously playing the guitar (who knew?) with a crowd, a legitimate crowd, on the deck of a freighter against some mod protest posters. He is both ecological and ego-logical.

Third: A Polaroid with an orangy glint; Dad is smiling so wide his face is distorted. He looks elastic. Which raises the question: When exactly was he ever that happy?

My fingers are cold. They're chattering.

"Yogo," I hear coming from the direction of Eb. "Yoga! Yogodayo!" At an alarmingly high volume, he seems to be yodeling. Or at least doing a weird vocalizing that makes my teeth hurt. Perhaps revealing he has Dad's covert musical talent.

"Take him," I yell to Fern from Dad's office. I put the envelope back, vacant, into the sweet-smelling box and close the lid. Next time I'll search for the source of the sugariness. I could use, we all could use, a hit of the weed.

Gussy scrambles up and scuttles out of the room. Latent poodle intelligence at work.

Back in the still-radiant kitchen, I put on an apron—STOP GLOBAL WARMING!—and tuck the pictures in the front pocket. The images are together, right sides facing in. The strangers are kissing, for all I know. It's getting chilly. I throw on Maris's old cashmere cardigan hanging on the pantry doorknob.

Fern meets me at the kitchen table with Eb spilling out of her arms, still braying. She pinches him hard, and I don't say anything. When Fern's turn comes, she will make a good mother. Better than Maris, certainly. Better possibly than me.

Chloe slams out the screen door, a pencil clenched between her teeth. She knows when and how to go home four doors down.

Noah sets the table. Candles, cloth napkins, a spatterware pitcher filled with water. He kisses me good-bye—shortish—before joining his father for a quick take-out dinner. Ever since the divorce (hmm, could that be a tipping point with Susannah?—come back to this thought), he spends Monday through Wednesday on-island with his father and Thursday through Sunday in Portland with his mother.

Now that we're back to the original cast of *Charlotte's Web*, we shift into serious cooking mode. I sit Eb on the counter. He watches the water run through the garbanzos as I lift the colander up and down so it rains in the sink. Fern pulls over the creaky ladder-back chair and compulsively peels carrots, scraping three times, then turning, scraping, then turning. She clucks her tongue to some tune in her head. Potentially, "The Farmer in the Dell."

This is, I figure, normal neurotic behavior in a four-year-old. I was legendary for laundry folding, smoothing pillowcases with my hands and then creasing them into insanely perfect squares. I press the apron pocket where Dad's happy face hides.

Time to crank the music. Even before hatching my lobster escape plan, I'd taken on the important job of teaching Fern and Eb lyrics to certain essential songs. A bent and bitter soundtrack seems a good childhood legacy. Even if they grow up and like some saccharine-sixteen girl, they'll know every warped word of "Psycho-Killer." Hopefully, they will not come to associate this ditty with their daddy. In fact, Talking Heads is at volume nine when Simon/Si walks through the back door into the kitchen.

"Where's the mail?" he asks. "Anything good?" Is he expecting a warrant? He comes too close to me and my photos of him.

"Nothing for you," I say.

He presses his nose to the thermostat so he can read the tiny dial. "Did you flick this up?"

"Set the heat to ninety degrees like I always do." Never do, for the record.

"If you're cold, put on a sweater."

"Dad, I'm wearing a sweater. I'm always wearing a sweater. I didn't touch the thermostat. I'm not complaining."

He turns to me. "You always wear a sweater?"

"Or a fleece, sometimes a fleece."

"I guess it's your mother who gets cold."

I hand him an onion to chop. He'll do a sloppy job, but it doesn't matter. Couscous is pretty un-screw-up-able.

By the time Maris rolls in, the four of us are sitting at the table in our sweaters. "Very nice ballet posture," she offers me. That's the way to get to Maris, through culture.

"*Merci,*" I say. Little does she know I'm sitting up straight so as not to spill on the pocket of the apron with the purloined photos.

Damned if the meal, on real plates I'll later have to wash, isn't perfect. I keep the conversation afloat, swooping into any silence with a mention of the Solstice. Even Eb joins in with a little yodel. At some point I notice Mom and Dad are talking—but not to each other. I take a forkful of pine nut and feta—it's an inspired flavor combination. Yum. By the time it gets to the back of my throat, though, it's sour as a bastard.

Two (c)

I take the apron off to do the dishes—the secret photos now tucked in my secret lobster folder—and thread my arms back through the cardigan.

While sudsing with lemon verbena soap at the kitchen sink, I face out to the family room and, indeed, the family. To the madness that is Dadness.

True, everyone who moves to an island is a little psycho. Nikki's family, to take one bizarro example, is starting an umbrella cover collection—you know those little sheaths that fit over umbrellas? They've got about three hundred so far. I couldn't make this up.

Maris is odd exactly because in another place she'd be so perfectly normal. In a Bleak land of overalls and wool clogs, she's all pencil skirts and pointy pumps. No one looks like her—toting legal briefs on the ferry, keeping to herself, perched sparrowlike inside a birdcage of her own making. Even her little unscripted stay at the psych facility is a city conceit—who on-island has the luxury of taking ten days off for anxiety?

Dad always rolls his eyes about her insanely good taste, but he can't dupe me, the queen of the eye roll. Besides, he turns all weirdly proud when the two of them have the (rare) dinner party and he finds a way to bring up how she once won some Wellesley-girl-of-the-year award and got interviewed on a dull morning show seen in ten homes.

He'll say, "Where is that old videotape?" He'll scooch his chair back from the table and pretend to not know where to look. Then he'll fish the tape out from under a leaning tower of literary paperbacks. "Well, ah. Here," he'll say, fooling no one.

The video is grainy, and she closes her eyes when she talks. Still, you can see who she'll grow up to be— that groomed but brainy type, maybe a food writer who specializes in cheeses of the Rhône. Or a lawyer. I guess that works too. On the screen her hair is too big and her shirt is too loud.

Even so, she's pretty watchable. He's still watching, isn't he?

"Up for a game?" Simon asks. It's not clear who he is hoping will bite. (Too bad Chloe the biter isn't still over.) We're all mute. "Well, good thing Lola is always up for a game," he says, sinking into the sofa with Lola the laptop.

I take the old green linen towel, my favorite, and hold it to my cheek for a second. It's soft and worn. No dishwasher for us; no unnecessary production of carbon emissions.

Then the front door cracks open and a ribbon of cold air blows in.

"Oh, hello, Noah," Maris says. "Children, please greet Noah."

Like the sibs don't greet Noah ten times a day. Like he wasn't already here. Like they don't already love him.

Noah slants into me, waiting for me to finish drying. He leans the way Gussy leans—in all trust, with all weight. He is wonderfully warm. He is August.

"Air?" I ask. He flings both thumbs up, a dweeb move, but I don't give a flying fug.

"Noah, you look well," Maris says. She's not even looking at him.

Yes, let's get out where the sky is clear and sincere.

I grab a hoodie from its peg in the mudroom. We hold hands down the porch steps, Noah's thumb tight against my palm, and find our way across the irregular stones through the yard.

The skeletons of the vegetable garden glimmer in the light of the *demi-lune*. It won't be time to plant until early June. There is no spring here. We go right from muddy snow to fragile summer. I tell the siblets that

66

lettuces and radishes are gnome-grown, that's how magical it seems when the sun finally settles in and pushes vegetables out of the ground. I shove away the thought that next summer I may be coming back after being away all year, just another seasonal casualty.

Destination: the macramé hammock we bought Dad a few moons back. As far as I know, he's never set ass in it. But then how much do I even know about Si/Simon/Dad?

I lie down first, and Noah lowers himself over me, like he's doing a push-up. This doesn't work well on the macramé/slack-ramé, and he collapses. Our lips smash together. We give in to gravity and make out. For a long time. I take a Noah taste, then another, and another. This is nothing new, of course, but it feels newish, since I'm mentally counting down the days until I make a run for it. Tick.

He tugs on the strings of my hoodie. "Let's take this off." Something must feel newish to him too.

"It's seven degrees," I say.

"Cold is a state of mind."

"Cold is a state of Maine."

What the fug? Once I tell him about boarding school, he might stop speaking to me, let alone touching me.

I slip the sweatshirt over my head along with the sweater, long-sleeved tee, thermal tank, lacy cami, and, finally, purple bra. (Little fashion maggie tip: Big bras in fun colors don't look so granny!) We've been close to this place before. But not quite. Not quite so nakedly here.

Noah folds my hoodie (yep, he's a neatnik), lifts me up, and puts it under my ass. We have positive pelvic contact. We are cartographers. We are two topographical maps, all contours and valleys.

The sky is cloudless. There are stars, entire constellations, looking down on us.

I wrap around his waist. A *grand plié* in second position. My very short legs somehow fit just fine around Noah's very fine ass. For the hell of it, I point my toes. Somewhere Miss Sascha, my ex-ballet instructor, would be proud.

I chatter.

"Cold?" whispers Noah. He's taken off his shirt too. He's rubbing my arms, trying to erase the goose bumps.

"In a good way."

We produce heat and friction and other hypothermia-preventative measures for many brilliant minutes. That wax-ripped bald spot at the verge of my crotch thumps.

"I love this. Love you," he says. He's said it before. I'm stingier with the mush. Consider saying something other than "ditto." Consider saying I love you so much I worry I won't leave you and then I'll waste my life and never escape Lobsterland, a place that could actually not care less about me.

This is why I say nothing. Can you imagine what would happen if I actually said even ten percent of the things I think? I'd be the one just out of the residential facility, not Maris.

Then, right on cue, "Char," the wet blanket calls, "I don't see the children's lunches." Mom's voice is minor and far away. I know she won't come outside. She's not an outdoor type.

Still, it breaks the frame.

Noah rehooks my bra. He says warm and fuzzy things about my pendulous (Wordly Wise Word!) breasts, which, until ten minutes ago, he had only seen poking out of a polka-dot bikini in his mom's hot tub in Portland.

I yank the shirt(s) over my head. Suddenly, I'm glacial. He finds his chamois shirt, and I kiss-button-kiss-button it up for him.

Noah heads home to his father's house, and I take a seriously deep breath before swinging open the backdoor and reentering the fray. I don't even look at Maris. Noah—not the actual person but his residual warmth—is alongside me, the memory of his thumb on my palm. It feels like together we take the turkey, the avocado, the provolone, the sprouts from the purring fridge. On multigrain bread with sunflower seeds, I/we make the siblets sandwiches to write home about.

Two (d)

Our old shingle house doesn't have anything as ordinary or useful as a lock on the bedroom door. So I wedge my desk chair—painted unmellow yellow—under the porcelain knob, my version of DO NOT DISTURB.

I squint through half-shut eyes into the full-length mirror on the back of the closet door trying to half see what Noah sees in me. Moonlight streams through the windows, throwing shadows. I suck in my stomach. *Suck* being the operative word. I need less boobage and longer legs. Susannah has the sunken-model thing going for her. She is concave in the best possible way, plus she trolls the high school halls in jeans she doesn't have to shorten, jeans that don't look like they ate her feet.

Here is the ideal body math: one smaller cup size = three inches leg length. If I could shrink to a C, I'd suddenly be five foot three. That's a bargain I'd make. Bring on Mephistopheles.

Then again, the height differential didn't much get in the way tonight when I was horizontal in the hammock with Noah. And, anyway, when I lie down, it's possible my boobs pancake out enough to be in the normal range.

At least I have good hair—long and coppery and wavy. Impartial evidence: When the superfluously lettered Thom tried to feel me up at Homecoming, he whispered, "I want to part your hair with my tongue." Although seriously ew, it stuck in my brain because, face it, it's a compliment.

Anytime I'm feeling repulsive, I think, well, there's some guy who wants to make out with my part. Sad.

Enough procrastination. I put on Rufus Wainwright—way unappreciated. Best song ever: "Cigarettes and Chocolate Milk." I've only smoked once (okay, nine times), and I don't even like dairy (who does?). Still, Rufus is a genius boy.

Try short-answer question number four:

PLEASE SHARE WITH US THE EXTRACURRICULAR ACHIEVEMENTS ABOUT WHICH YOU ARE ESPECIALLY PROUD OR PASSIONATE. USE ADDITIONAL PAPER IF NECESSARY.

Sloppy copy:

Additional paper will not be necessary. In fact, I have no idea how I'm going to fill this space at all.

Okay, breathe. I'm proud that I read the paper, really read the paper. That's become a key extracurricular activity—better than the dweeby Key Club, don't you think? I know you expect me to write about lacrosse or even water polo, a sport on the rise with good scholarship opportunities, according to my guidance counselor. And I could fake a sport or adopt one if it would help. That's how desperate I am to go to a school, your school, that isn't my school.

I can tell you I used to be into drama, especially musical theater. If you were to look at the Mainely Drama Web site (which is a really moronic site, so I'm not recommending it) you'd see I had bitty bit parts in Oklahoma *and* Pippin. *Never really found my corner of the sky, unless you count tonight outside with my boyfriend. We didn't find a corner so much as a whole fugging galaxy. Oh, I also used to do ballet. I had a pretty plié and I stayed with it long enough to go on pointe before I thought, Really, what's the point?*

If you want to know the naked truth, I was mediocre. And naked truth number two, I don't have a dancer body (the bra debacle, for starters). I assume you are all punctilious readers, so I also assume you've picked up on the tense here.

As in past. I gave up these extracurriculars—my extra-c's—when I was twelve. Which happened to coincide with the birth of my little girl, followed three years later by the birth of my baby boy.

Notice how I say my. They are mine in the sense that I take care of them. No one tells me that I have to, and for a while we had weirdo Mrs. Gray, who always, but I mean always, wore a sailor's cap. (She was Captain and fugging Tenille.)

I don't mean to sound pathetic. Or apathetic. I'm sure you hate apathy.

I have a good role model when it comes to car-ing about this world. Pick a cause, any cause, and my father has fought for it. Protecting the ancient forests of Newfoundland. Check. Boycotting Coca-Cola for its role in the nasty malnourishment caused by Fanta Baby Syndrome. Check.

So why do I drink a Coke every day, you ask? I'd go with simple rebellion, but the real question is why has Dad's passion lost its fizz? Why has it morphed from eco-activism into an obsession with a nearly sixty-year-old word game? (Eight letters: Scrabble.)

Does it mean he is guilty or not guilty of hav-ing his elbow on America's Most Wanted? Does it mean it's his word, his letters, against mine?

Mr. (AP Lit) Trice says to close with a kicker, so here it is: I feel passionate about understanding my father, the somewhat wanted.

That whiplash truth makes me fling my door back open. The chair topples over from its sentry place. I can't wait to get back downstairs, to be un-alone. I can't wait to spend time with the siblets I love. I'll even take time with the parents I hate.

Two (e)

Maris is the only one awake. Lucky me. She sits in the shadows of the chintz love seat, a faded glory she's had since childhood. I flash back on this morning's self-promise: to have a real conversation with a family member over the age of four. Tick. I stay on the bottom stair, undetected, until I figure out what to say.

That love seat was in her bedroom when she was my age. Maris grew up in a la-di-dah house with beamed ceilings and a million panes of glass. When we visit, I take the perfect-youth tour: framed photos of her with horses, with poodles, with a procession of tanned dates. The photos stop somewhere around the age of Dad. Dad who? He's never in the picture.

If I was Noah, and I am so not, I would look into Maris's eyes and say, "Something's been troubling me, and I need your wisdom." He would totally do this queer thing. I love him anyway, and not just because there are only ten teenage guys on the island (twelve, if you count the two in juvie).

For some random reason, I think of the doctor at the Eye Guy holding those giganto clicky circles over my eyes when I needed new glasses. He switched between two possible prescriptions and asked the same question two million times. Better or worse? Better or worse? Better to talk to her or worse? Better.

"Evening, Mom," I say from the doorway, starting without a script. I can always claim homework if she looks crazy. When I get closer, I see she's not wearing a shirt. She still has her stockings on, and her charcoal skirt, but she's in a dingy ivory bra. She's nursing the dregs of her sulfite-free Pinot. She's a glass half empty.

Her feet are tucked under her, little red notebook in hand, making a to-do list she'll never do. She's a list maker, not a list doer. There are stacks of lists around the house—torn out and thrown away. I vow not to do that with my apps. Vow not to fill them out for sport and never follow through.

I fixate on the top of her head so as not to seem pervy. "Mom, is there anything you want to talk about?"

Immediately, I want to rephrase, because what she wants to talk about, possibly, is herself. How we thought she was having a heart attack last month when she collapsed in court. How when the bailiff came to her side she told him—screamed at him, apparently—that the walls were closing in and her heart was busting out of her chest and her legs were like lime Jell-O. She really said lime Jell-O, not just generic Jell-O; that's how exacting she is, even in distress. How I then thought it would be better if she'd had a real heart attack—something that can be fixed—than land herself in Casco Hills for ten days with shitloads of antianxiety pills for company.

"Follow-up," I add quickly, like some idiotic White House reporter. "Is there anything *about Dad* you want to tell me?"

She looks up but doesn't answer. Her silence is an invitation for me to fill the void. This is a mean lawyer trick—stay quiet long enough and the witness will hang herself. Better or worse to keep quiet? Worse.

"Is there something I should know about Dad and his past?" It sounds melodramatic, but at the moment I don't give a shiitake, holy or otherwise.

She gives a big exhale, like the smoker she was. It seems she's gearing up, as if she's anticipated this very query. Leave it to a lawyer.

"It's time you know the full story" is what she says, taking my hand.

Look, Ma, a maternal gesture.

"Okay, then." I brace for bad news: He's wanted in twenty-two states! Or for good: I'm the crazy one for doubting that the man who taught me how to steer a sailboat into the wind might have earned the mocking Unabomber moniker.

"He was among the first people I slept with. But I'm clearly not his last."

The floor is on the move. It's water. She looks at me, prepared to share more. Better or worse to let her keep going?

Better. I nod. And sit—sink, really—straight down.

"Let's see," she says, as though scanning a mental— or could it be a literal?—list. She may have made this list of his infractions in her notebook. "Berjan was the first. The first I found out about anyway."

"Berjan?" I ask, from way down on the floor. The preschool teacher, the same perfect teacher I scooped Eb from this afternoon? Ew. I hadn't thought through the cause-and-effect here. If I ask her out loud, she can answer out loud.

She continues. "Then there was Kat. Don't know what he saw in that." Kat? KAT! Who was arrested for growing weed behind her studio one road over? "Remember that time he was working on a software launch and had to, quote, stay in Portland, unquote?" Mom asks. "That was Kat."

My head bobs up, rooting around for air. There is no air in this house. Or there's too much, the cold, drafty kind you can't catch.

"I only thought he might be a criminal," I say in little gasps. "Is there someone new? Someone now?" Pause. "Is that why you needed—" Rephrase. "Is that why you were more comfortable in the hospital?" That was what the emergency room doctor apparently asked, "Would you be more comfortable in a hospital?"

"Well, of course. Adultery is against the law," Maris says. Note how she didn't really answer my question— the one that started the conversation or the one that ended it. People think lawyers are so clever, but if you have a parent-barrister you know the truth. Law is hockey. It's about defending your goals.

I unlock from looking at Maris and the flood beneath my ass recedes. I actually feel my feet under me. I walk to the window and find Dad. He's in the front yard, out by himself (again), looking at stars (again).

"I can see this is a lot to take in," she says finally, uncrossing her longer-than-mine legs and standing. She wraps the mohair throw around her thin shoulders. Now she covers up.

For whatever regressive reason, I flip my ponytail to the front and suck on the end. With each stair, I stuff more hair down my throat.

And think: Worse. Definitely worse.

Two (f)

Even though it's midnight, I am not close to sleep. I can't get the taste of my hair, or my mother, or my Noah, out of my head. It's too many flavors, too strange a cocktail, to try to swallow.

Surely, Maris has tucked in by now, tuckered out from her truth telling or her wine swilling or both. The house is morgue quiet when I go back downstairs. The TV isn't on the kitchen counter anymore—she probably took Letterman to bed.

I pour a glass of cider. Unfiltered, of course. Can't anything in this house be clear? And then I get the lightbulb: I'll leave.

We keep a musty old van on-island (unlike Maris's hybrid, which is parked at a lot in Portland). Technically, I'm not supposed to drive without an adult in the car—but who is more adult in this house than me?

I snatch the keys from the back hook and get outside fast over the brittle walk.

With my sheepskin slipper, I push in the clutch of the '83 Plymouth (the rare year a minivan had a manual transmission) and coax the motor over, willing it to be quiet. It cooperates. The streets are blank. Bleak, indeed. Only the Duncans and the Guthries—both awayers—have lights on, aglow from within, jack-o'-lantern style.

I'd love to get lost. But there's no way to lose yourself on an island. The water is always the compass.

The primordial Plym van heads to the dock, as if on autopilot. And why not? Perhaps I'll run into Hunky Henry the ferry boy. The boat always spends the night island-side, just in case Mr. Millard (or whoever) has an actual, factual heart attack and needs a run over to Maine Med.

The boat is asleep at the slip. Still, I get out and walk to the lip of the bay and, beyond that, the Atlantic. Through the planks I can see the water on the move. It's dizzying. And freezing. Must be four degrees.

Ideally, I'd be wearing something other than thermal pajamas. I look across the water, and guess what? No. One. Is. There.

Back in the warm(er) van, I switch on the dash light only to find, of course, that I am alone here too. Whoever wrote "No man is an island" (John Donne, I think) never spent a winter on Bleak. I poke around the family Plym in search of company. Odd bits of breakfast bars, half-full water bottles, uncapped pens, dog treats that have gone MIA, a pair of scissors, old hair elastics, a lone ballet slipper. There's a British home magazine jammed near the gearshift. Damned if the English don't have a way with color—love the partnership of chocolate brown and robin's-egg blue.

Maybe I'll go to Oxford instead of the Sorbonne. By the time I'm in graduate school in one foreign place or the other, the siblets and I will be the same age. I will stop getting older and they will catch up. They'll be what I am now, which is essentially grown up. Seriously, how much older will I ever feel?

I crank up the old van to head back home to my fellow islands—my family archipelago—but the engine stutters. Putt. More like pffft. This is not in the plan—if there was a plan. This is life telling me I can't un-Bleak in the blink of an eye.

So I get out, subscribing to the deluded theory that sometimes, if you don't push and prod, problems just fix themselves.

Back to the water. I've never been one of those polar people who swim in the Atlantic on New Year's Day just because it's possible. But tonight I dip a toe in and the water doesn't bite.

I look back to shore thinking for one stupid moment that Maris or Dad may have noticed that I'm gone, that the van is gone, and run down to the dock to make sure we are safe. To make sure I haven't killed the car and possibly myself. Really, how hard would it be to slip on these rocks and fall to a tragic death? Then I snap out of it because I don't want to be a tortured type who thinks life sucks so very much that moping and medicating are necessary. No one likes a suicide girl. And anyway, who am I kidding? I am *über*-sure-footed. I could traverse these shoals in heels.

Fug it. I reverse myself over the razory rocks and find a towel in the van's way-back. This time the motor kicks right over, and I head home. It was an ignore-it-and-it-gets-better scenario after all.

Total time gone: forty minutes. Is that enough? Enough for what, who knows, but I'm just asking. I pee in the downstairs bathroom so the flush won't wake anyone.

Dad is sacked out on the love seat, his feet over-hanging the chintz arm. Wonder if Maris gave him the boot. He's got a glass of water next to him. Tonight, he is the glass half full.

I check on the sibs. Fern fiercely holds her stuffed elephant (please God, don't let her grow up to be a Republican). Eb snuffles like he may be coming down with something. I should paint their room—the yellow has an unfortunate resemblance to Eb's post-oatmeal poo. Why not green—celery or grass or sage?

As I whirl the color wheel of my mind, I realize it's out there, the person I've become: a shirt-snatcher, a photo-snooper, a prepster-poser, a pathetic sixteen-year-old virgin obsessed with color.

WEDNESDAY

Three (a)

Another day, another trauma, albeit minor compared to last night's maternal fiasco. I make Eb cry. I stuff him into his red gingham snowsuit and zip it up harshly, drawing a freckle of blood on his chin. This morning I'm the bad mother, I'm the one inflicting pain. I give him a teensy kiss but don't have time to dwell.

Besides, we're late. I grab a Tupperware, throw in some cranberry granola, toss a hunk to Gussy (better oats than Prozac), fill the plaid thermos with soy milk, slip Eb's red Keds into my pocket, and head for the 7:05.

The dock is half a mile down a long, low hill—nine minutes or so, depending on how slick the streets are and how steady we are on our feet. Today: very and not very, respectively. There's a light rain. If the temperature drops another five degrees, we're talking white stuff.

"A ride, *s'il vous plaît*," Fern says. She's a big four, but who gives.

"Hop on." She wedges her ladybug boots above the stroller's back wheels and seizes the handles. I keep a tight grip downhill so she doesn't gather too much mojo.

When we get to the last dip in the hill, past the peeling-paint house that will be gleaming by June 1, in time for the summer folk, I spot a speck of Noah standing on deck. He waves wildly, trying to reel us in.

It's weird to see him in daylight all bundled up instead of in moonlight all not.

We three sibs step on board as the horn blares. I dump my book bag on the metal floor of the lower deck and fish out breakfast.

"I better come over again tonight. To study," Noah says, kissing my top lip. "You are quite the study buddy."

"I could be more. I could be your fucky buddy," I say just loud enough to be swallowed by the wind. I stifle a yawn. Gussy yawns when she's nervous. Maybe I'm jumpy about leaving my buddy (study/fucky/lucky). It feels very in-between. Just as I have naked contact with the love of my life, or at least my island, I am on the verge of ditching them both. This would probably be the time to mention that I plan to haul ass off to boarding school.

I look up to see Hunkaman Henry looking right back at me. He hoists his thermos in my direction. With a nod of the soy milk, I toast back: *L'chaim!*

"Are we on?" Noah asks.

"Very on," I say. So it's not the right time to share. "Turned completely on." The morning mist thickens as we approach Portland. The air is crème brûlée without the crust, without the good part. My hair frizzes in response. Soon I'll have the Maine mane, an unfortunate halo of 'fro. "Why wouldn't we be on?" I say, smacking my hair over my ears, willing it into submission. Noah doesn't hear me. He kneels down in his old corduroys to say morning to the siblets.

I pull out two bowls tucked under the stroller seat and fill one with cranny granny and the other with infant-friendly organic Cheerios. Fern and Eb sit knee-to-knee on the ledge, spoons in hand, little spades digging in the garden of organic delights. I lean into Noah, my back to his front, and daydream in the deep blue bay.

I flash on the myth (fact?) that for ten thousand years the Lobster Goddess was said to rule this bay, carving the shoreline of the islands with her claw. As legend has it, she made Bleak on the last day of her reign and then slipped, quite permanently, into the bay. Either saved the best for last or killed herself, depending on your level of sarcasm.

"Speaking of the Lobster Goddess," I say over my shoulder.

"Were we?" Noah asks.

"In my head we were. Can we go to the Solstice dance late this year? I've got something to do at five." Unsaid: I have to mail the apps. The nerve endings in my fingers tingle as I think about the cold metal mail chute snapping shut. "Why don't we turn up at six. Or seven. Or we could skip the whole thing."

I pivot to face him on today's heels, brown boots with the smallest bit of nontacky fringe.

"Listen, I'll meet you there." He looks down, exposing the freckles on his eyelids.

"That's a fast answer."

"Susannah asked me to walk in with her. Just so she's not alone."

I whip my head around half expecting to see the Goddess-to-be, but no. Oh, Susannah can sleep in and catch the next boat because she doesn't have to do the day-care drill.

"So I'll be alone," I say, flashing back to my solo semiswim last night at the island's edge. "Better I walk in alone. Makes perfect sense." I sound like a Jewish grandmother. I sound like my Jewish grandmother. I hover over the bench, keeping my face to myself, pretending to see if the siblets need a granola refill.

Really, why shouldn't he kill time with Susannah while I'm plotting my escape from him, from her, from the whole Bleak population of five hundred (and growing)? Like I said, in between, in between, in between.

"Why that look?" he asks. "It's not like you're running for Lobster Goddess. Not that you couldn't. But she needs an escort."

I put my hand over my leg, which has chosen to betray my calm façade and syncopate. The Lobster Goddess story is probably a marketing ploy anyway, the brainchild (brinechild) of the local jeweler who takes out charming little ads in the back of the *New Yorker* with the narrative printed up alongside his island bracelets.

"Hey, Henry," I say, doing a jig thing to keep my leg calm. I hop in his direction. "Give me your vote. Is there such a thing as a Lobster Goddess?"

"Nah." He grins. I see his gloves in my peripheral vision. Better or worse, as the Eye Guy would ask? He leans over me and puts up my hood. When his gloves are up by my eyes, he whispers so softly I can barely hear him. "If there was a goddess, she would free the lobsters. No crustacean ruler would tolerate her subjects being caught and eaten—and in drawn butter, no less." He's got quite a nice smile.

"If I were the goddess," I say to him in only a slightly louder voice, "I would be a liberator. If the lobsters want out, by all means let them go." I beam back, though I know for a fact that my smile falls short. In this moment, I realize I truly trust Noah. Trust is when you smile for someone even though you know your eyes disappear into your face. Even though showing happiness makes you look deformed.

We're within spitting distance of the Portland dock. Henry takes the stairs three at a time, stationing himself by the pier, in lasso position. Noah helps the siblets dump the dregs of the granola in the compost bin near the regular garbage. Fern wipes out the bowls with the bandana she keeps tied to her turtle backpack. I'll have to wash that thing tonight. She whispers something I can't hear to Eb. He claps his sticky mitties.

I say to Noah, "Before we study, we better talk." I could just say it now, blurt it out, and he'd have all day to get used to the idea and all night to kiss and make up. And more.

But—boom, boom, boom—we dock and Henry lashes us to the land. Saved, or lost, by that fugging horn.

Three (b)

Forget lunch (it's always forgettable). I smack into Susannah in the main hallway on the way to the library. Sorry, the media center.

"You have got to see this," she says, throwing her backpack on the linoleum and pawing through it a little frantically. She gets a new Beans bag each September—spoiled even before the divorce—and each year she chooses the most noxious color available. Meet Camouflage Kiwi.

"I'm not sure my piano legs want to." I picture Susannah's glittery nail flipping me off. I could do the same—return the finger or go ahead and say fuck you—but there's no winning with Susannah. Just kissing and making up, which we used to do quite literally—kissing each other's noses and then playing with her mom's giant stash of makeup. "What is it, anyway?"

"I made this for Noah. Do you think he'll like it?" She shakes a CD like a leaf. "I call it 'Noah-man.' Like the Beatles song," she says. Worse, she sings. "He's a real Noah-man. Sitting in his Noah-land. Making all his Noah-plans for Noah-body."

"He'll hate it." Why do people even say shake like a leaf? Leaves fall. They drift. My mind drifts to Susannah sitting on her thick carpet in her skinny camisole, scrolling through her download library for my boyfriend.

"Wrong-o. He'll love it. You don't know him as well as you think you do," she says, stabbing that nail in the air for emphasis. The polish has chipped since Monday.

Not that I'd say so out loud, but she could be right about the not-knowing part. And it raises the obvious question: Do I know anyone as well as I think I do?

Rewind to a time—four years ago or so—I'd have bet my braid that Dad would be on the cover of *Wired* for inventing some genius software. I loved the boho in him, loved that the Plymouth was plastered with bumper stickers: "Don't Californicate Maine," "My Poodle Is Smarter Than Your Honor Student," "Friends Don't Let Friends Vote Republican."

Fast forward to the present. Dad's slacker clothes have crossed the line from quirky to dirty. Literally one pair of khakis! And the intense Scrabble-ology is somewhere north of pathetic.

I'm mad at my twelve-year-old self for not realizing just how good I had it. Before the siblets—before Mom's fondness for Pinot and her need for psychedelic-colored pharmaceuticals, and before the island seemed like it would smother any whit of creativity—life was actually fine.

Or I didn't know it could be better, which is really the same thing as it being good.

Evidence of how I avoid Dad now: I never ask him to open a jar. He'll say, "Where is the jar-opener gizmo?" I'll have no idea, and he'll slam through a few drawers and find the unopened gas bill mixed in with the high school handbook and say, "I don't know why your mother doesn't buy green electricity." It's easier to just put the jar of salsa back on the shelf and not make guacamole. Even though I'm a guacaholic (without cilantro).

I look around the media center from my perch by the periodicals and think, I'd paint these walls pink, but not psych-ward pink. That's a mighty grim pink they use in Casco Hills, Maris's hospital-away-from-home. No, the shade I have in mind is more like the delicate pink of the peonies that bloom just as it seems there will be absolutely no spring whatsoever. The color of hope.

"Charlotte?" Noah says, breaking the moment. He's standing behind me. (For how long? Did he see my head crooked in some lame-ass way looking at the paint?) His hand grips the back of the wooden chair like he might decide to pull it out.

He taps an envelope—hard—on top of my head, then throws it on the table. "Mr. Trice asked me to give you this recommendation. Are you crazy? I don't get it."

Focus on the size of Mr. Trice's envelope: thick. I hope he didn't add an essay as proof of my genius. Only among the Portlandy am I potentially brilliant.

"This too," says Noah. He stuffs his fist into his pocket and pulls out a rumpled purple Post-it from Mr. Trice. "If Lawrenceville doesn't take you, I'll sue. Love, Lars." Again with the Lars.

"Utterly insignificant," I say at hyperspeed. It sounds like "utternant," which could pass for one of Dad's obscure Scrabble words. "It is a joke. Ha! It is a complete could-I-get-in joke."

"For once, you are really not funny," he says.

A little tune starts up in my head from an old Squeeze CD: "I'd beg for your forgiveness, but begging's not my business." The muscles in my leg squeeze too. The leg-tapping bounces the fake wood table.

Out of the blue, I have a craving for nuts, preferably unsalted.

Then the tears (minor) start. I knock my thigh harder into the underside of the table. The thigh that was wrapped so utterly significantly around Noah last night. Now I want a bruise. "You know how much everything sucks."

"I didn't know we sucked." He doesn't move closer. He is so not close I'm afraid Ms. Libation/Librarian (everyone knows she packs a flask) will shush us. Besides, the not-suck part is debatable, what with the incendiary Susannah burning scorching CDs for him.

I stand up and kiss him right there in the should-be-pink library. This is huge because I've always been anti-PDA at school.

After all the delicious kisses of last night, a night I hope will launch a thousand other close (unclothed) encounters, it's surprisingly hard to connect lips. He's statue-still.

He pulls away. That's two times this week. "What are you doing, Charlotte?"

I'd consider telling him the truth, if only I knew it. I only get this much and it's really not much at all: I am a person divided, a person falling, spiraling.

Stay with me for a minute. They say a plane never crashes for a single simple reason. It takes a whole series of screwups—failures of things mechanical and human—to bring one of those hulks of steel spiraling to the ground.

Well, I second that emotion. It's not one thing. Not just my dad (criminal) or just my mom (psycho) or just my sibs (needy) or just my Noah (pissed). It's the whole series of failures, my whole series of failures.

In the twenty-two seconds it takes for my brain to hit this cul-de-sac, Noah's been staring at me with those gray eyes so gorgeous I couldn't make them up. "Hello," he says. "Take two. What are you doing?"

"I have no idea." I sit back down because I just may pass out if I don't. "I've got something for you," I say, rooting around my own Beans bag, the one I've had since fifth grade.

Out comes a small box wrapped in batik fabric. The siblets and I had a crafty Sunday—vats of wax, twine, kettles of vegetable dye—to make presents for the Solstice. It's yet another thing to love about the littles: They give me an excuse to spend a day with my elbows in wax.

"Open," I say, offering up the box on my palm, waitress-style, as if to say, Care to have one? "I was going to wait, but go ahead."

"I don't have anything for you," he says, shaking his head. His little bleached hunk swings. "I went shopping with Susannah. She wanted a boy opinion on her Lobster dress. But I didn't see anything. For you, I mean."

"Tremendous," I say, trying hard not to pout, seeing as I'm the guilt-ridden party at the moment.

"Except a Coke bottle," Noah adds. "One of those old-fashioned glass Coke bottles. I know you like those.

But it wasn't enough—not then." He leans over at an awkward angle. He's diagonal.

I slide the box down the smooth table. My pointer finger is still faintly violet from the dye.

He unwraps the fabric and tentatively opens the box.

"Ta da," I say, softly. It's a locket of two mussel shells, light as dust, held together with navy blue embroidery floss I oh-so-carefully threaded through the thickest part, the very heart, of the shell.

His mouth, his nose, his ears seem so exposed—jutting out into thin air, undressed. "I'll put your picture in it," he whispers. I can feel his breath near my silver hoop.

"Don't."

"When you leave, I mean."

"No, don't." My head whizzes with thoughts, and I try to outrun them with words. "Put it in a shoe box with the cigarettes we forgot to smoke and the condoms we forgot to use and all those summers' worth of Popsicle sticks we forgot to throw away." I flash on Dad's van and its forgot-to-throw-away contents. Flash on hokey jokes in faded ink on the sticky Popsicle sticks: "What does an elephant pack?" "A trunk."

"Look at it two years from now or twenty years from now and think, 'Who was that short girl with elephantine boobs who gave me this piece of shit?'"

"I'll look at it and think, 'This is from the girl I love but don't get.'"

What did he say? What did I say? "I didn't even come up with the idea of it myself. It's not original. I took it from a magazine."

"From the girl who can't take a compliment. I'll miss you."

"Not for long," I say.

I don't even watch his fine ass leave the library. The media center.

Three (c)

Another purple Post-it enters my view, this one flapping against the mangled gray of my locker. That's some nasty color contrast at work. From Noah: "Our study session cancelled, obviously. I'll be at Susannah's." A little symmetry there with the Post-its. Bad news breeds bad news.

I gather Fern and Eb from Small World and try to keep my eyes focused only on the smalls. My chin has a mind of its own. It lifts up to watch Berjan, the preschool diva, for any sign of betrayal.

The thought of her with Dad is almost incestuous (Wordly Wise Word!). But if I hover above myself for a second, there's something oddly logical about it too. She's more of a mother, more of an organic mother, than Maris. Organic in the sense of elemental and also, in this case, as in pesticide-free.

That extra minute of musing on my part means we've missed the 3:35. Gussy is the only one who might notice, but she's safe, a safe-and-sound hound seeing as Maris's mother lode of meds has yet to be replenished.

"Shall we get some movies?" I ask, rhetorically, really. A little pop-cult diversion is what I need to cheer myself up on this gloomy-gus day.

Fern hitches a ride on the stroller. We first glide-slide over to the post office to check the PO coffin. It's stuffed full with furniture catalogs, hospital bills, and, hallelujah, bulging envelopes of Maris's many medications, two-day-delivered from Canada.

Next stop, the Videodrome. A nearly empty aquarium by the window captivates the kinder. They are oblivious to living life in a fishbowl. That's what island life is, really—one giant, or medium-size, fishbowl. I was born to run (though I'm no Springsteen fan, except for "Thunder Road"), but what happens in a bowl? Like a goldfish, I am on an endless loop. I can only go in circles.

I pluck a video of Celtic folktales off the shelf (kids) and walk to the documentary aisle (*moi*). If I were more of a drinker, a cocktail would help cut through the fog in my heart. Maybe it's worth mixing up a little vodka tonic when I get home.

Random observation: A piece of Scotch tape (not the Staples brand but the original Scotch with the plaid dispenser) smells like a vodka T. I could just huff tape.

The siblets continue to be reeled in by the lone fish near the window. Deeper in the store, an independent video, *Eco-Heroes, Coast to Coast*, is calling. There is a brunette front and center on the cover, not as pretty as the Pale Chick in Dad's photos. But she wears the same smug smile in her mug shot. Her smug shot. Outside, snow thinks about falling.

People always say if you don't like the weather in Maine, wait five minutes and it will change. They say it in Saratoga and Santa Monica too. And I bet it's not true in those places either. I've waited sixteen years, and the sky seems absolutely the same to me.

The ferry ride is uneventful. Hunkaman isn't on board. I'm bored.

Boom, boom, boom, we traipse up the hill in the dark. I quickly veer into Caddy's to grab a chicken, a head of garlic, and a lemon. And a roll of tape for a little vicarious V&T, why not?

"Don't need granola?" asks nosy Norma, emitting her usual fumes.

"Bought it in town," I say. Liar that I am.

The house is freezing. I go from room to room to room, turning on every single light, willing it to look sunny. I'll flip three quarters of the lamps off before Simon comes home to avoid his energy-saving spiel.

Before I plug in the VCR (we'll get a DVD player

when hell freezes over or the south polar cap melts, whichever comes first), I put Eb down for his nap. Why put down? Sounds like a dog command. Why not tucked in? Vow to say I tuck Eb in for his nap tomorrow.

I set Fern up at the kitchen table with a pot-holder project—stretchy loops on metal teeth. Over, under, over, under. It will take her forever to finish, or at least an hour. She'll keep at it until it's perfect, fusspot in training.

"What's your favorite color?" she asks. "I mean today."

"Today," I say, "it's white." Still wishing for actual snow as opposed to the idea of snow.

She looks down. "That's not a real color."

White is actually the most genuine of colors, linked to light and innocence and all things unpolluted (and sterility and lab coats, but I close down that thought sequence). Simpler to simply say, "I also like green, but not bright. Like a pine."

"I like a pine," Fern says, copying my inflection.

While the video rewinds, I inexplicably dash outside to look at the very empty hammock under the pines.

Okay, who (aside from Simon) says TV is a waste of brain cells? I learn two worthy facts. First, Maine's twist on Greenpeace was called DEEP, aka Down East Environmental Protectors. They were a homegrown but well-armed group, wielding lead lobster traps, pummeling boats, disrupting nuclear facilities. Second, and quite unfortunately, DEEP was orgy-obsessed. Icky video shows naked protesters, limbs tangled, disconnected. Does this explain Dad's wandering eye, among other organs?

Fern comes in to have me finish off her row. She's woven a white-and-green plaid.

"Perfect," I tell her. I switch off the TV. Enough in the DEEP. It seems more interesting to intertwine pot-holder loops than to weave a possible Dad narrative.

"This is fun, actually," says Fern.

"It is," I say. "Just fun, not even actually." Mental bookmark: Use more three- and four-letter words around Fern to save her from feeling like I do now. To save her from seeming too smart, even if only to herself.

Zigzag the loops and think, There are warrants out for the arrest of six former members. DEEP or shallow, the video didn't say. What are the odds? What are his odds?

Zigzag and think, In Simon's defense, those radicals don't look familiar. They look oddly more normal than Dad. They cut their hair; Dad's is still shaggy. They drive SUVs; Dad clings to the Plymouth. On the other (guilty) side, one woman could possibly be Pale Chick, but it's hard to tell. She looks shorter, hair and all.

The one who may/may not be Pale Chick talked about oceans of hope. Is there hope in an ocean, especially when you're surrounded by it? I close my mousy-brown eyes to imagine what she means, but I see only waves spitting against the shore, scattering everyone's promises. Hope seems too much to expect, even of the boundless Atlantic.

Eb yodels awake, but today I'm at peace (ha!) with it. I lift him up, wash the goopies out of his eyes. Fern meets us in the kitchen. Gussy jangles over to join the party.

I bounce Eb on my hip and shove a pricked lemon up the chicken's ass (sounds pervy, but makes the most yummy lemon chicken). The minute the lemon lodges in place, I think about the eco-warriors stuffing a pipe bomb up the ass of a police car.

Dad comes busting through the mudroom door. He looks absolutely the same, no more or less culpable.

"Smells good in here," he says, taking Eb off my hands. "Where's the mail?"

"All junk. Including Mom's medication."

"Show a little compassion," he says. He doesn't really mean it. Or he means it globally, show compassion for overexploited fish, but he doesn't mean show compassion to his wife, the pain-in-the-ass attorney.

While I wash the greens, Simon takes Eb to the family room. I can't see Dad, just his feet, sticking out from behind him. My guess is that he's lying on his stomach, nose to nose with the irresistible Eb. Was I, at one uncynical point, irresistible myself? I bore into his heel with my contact-dehydrated eyes (so Dad says I'm vain, it's not a crime) to see if his secret self has clung to the fuzzy wool socks they call Wicked Good at Beans.

My own eyes scratch me. I vow never to say "wicked" unless referring to the Witch of the West.

Okay, best line of *Rent*, the best musical ever: "Why Dorothy and Toto went over the rainbow? / To blow off Auntie Em! . . . *La Vie Bohème*."

Who do I need to blow off? Who does he?

I've torn the vitamin-filled mesclun greens into shreds. And anyway, his socks are silent.

Three (d)

Back in the shelter of my Cumulus Cotton–blue attic, I pull up the same chair I've been using for my app ramblings. I've grooved a little ass curve into the azure pillow. I'm surprised I haven't worn the blue off the wall, too, in the eye-level spot where I've been looking, drilling for inspiration.

Cue up Erase Errata. Noisy, post-fem, post-punk. Bonus points for being obscure at least on my obscure island.

Short-answer question number five:

IF THERE WERE ONE PERSON FROM HISTORY YOU COULD MEET, WHO WOULD IT BE AND WHAT WOULD YOU DISCUSS?

Sloppy copy:

I'd want to meet Sara Jane Olson, née Kathleen Soliah. You may have to look this one up, because I did. I came across her name while I was Internet-

searching (I know, the Internet isn't a proper research tool—but it got me started) to find out whether my father is a fugitive. And, by the way, if he is a fugitive (the jury is still out—not a literal jury, don't worry), does that improve my chances of being accepted? Does an applicant with a fugitive father count as an underrepresented minority?

In case you need reminding, Sara Jane is now in jail for life, found guilty of plugging pipe bombs up the tailpipe of a squad car. It took the FBI twenty years to find Sara Jane because she changed her name, changed her ways. She was living a perfectly ordinary life in Minneapolis with three daughters. The Feds pulled her over in her Plymouth minivan, a newer model, no doubt, than we have rusting in the driveway.

It's no small comfort to discover that my father apparently goes by two names.

Here's what I'd ask her kids: Was she manically into Scrabble? Did you find odd pictures of her with people you'd never seen? If you had skeevy thoughts, did you ever ask her about them? How?

The pen stops flying along because I have a sinking-thought intrusion. Am I making up a drama, a terrorist-trauma tale, as an excuse for Dad's slothful emotional life?

I open the lobster folder and take out the pictures

I pilfered from his office. Maybe Pale Chick is just a nondescript college girlfriend, a Yalie baby. Maybe I'm reading too much into his current detachment—it might mean he is just like me. Or that he loves his own company more than he loves Maris. Or the rest of us.

Then I file away the picture, and the thought.

That what-now part leads me to my runner-up choice: Ted Kaczynski's brother. This is not only because my father's scruffy look has earned him the unfortunate Unabomber nickname. You know who turned poor Ted in, right? His brother. His own family.

Life is long. It takes forever to get to the end of something. In Dad's case, I guess, twenty-six years. Back to the Kaczynski boys. You probably know what happened in Ted's brother's case. Seems like a happy ending now: Ted, safely behind bars, his brother safely clear of conscience. But what if that's not the last of it? What if the brother turns around and kills himself? It happens. It happened to the guy who helped rescue that girl stuck in a well. Remember that? One day the rescuer is a hero; a year later he's a failure, a deadly failure. What kind of ending would that be?

If I knew, absolutely knew, my father did something illegal, who would I tell? Who would he? Is this why he stays married to Maris, for free legal advice? I most certainly wouldn't, under any circumstance, contact the comb-over host from America's Top Ten Wanted. *Pleasy, so cheesy. But if I keep it to myself, will I have the woulda/shoulda/couldas forever?*

What I don't write is this: If I keep it to myself, will I, will we all, live irrevocably ever after?

Three (e)

I can half hear Dad reading the siblets a bedtime book in their ruthlessly mustard yellow bedroom. "Two Babar stories," Fern says.

"Two it is," says Dad. With the littles he is not a terrible father. I'll give him that.

Mom sits at the kitchen table, a pile of catalogs and bills in front of her, glass of red wine cradled in her hand. Looks like she got a manicure today—*mon dieu*, she eez well groomed.

On a very clear night I can glimpse the water from the left side of the kitchen sink. But not tonight. I concentrate on wrapping the leftover chicken—a wayward wing and thigh—in plastic wrap. Fern begged me to buy the crystal azure Saran. Simon doesn't approve of carcinogen-inducing polymers—he favors reusable Tupperware. He once (twice) threw a Tupperware party on-island. We have a set of matching "cake keepers" as hostess gifts. I use the last of the verboten Saran now. It looks sapphire in the places where I fold it over twice. This color thing is getting sad.

Out of the blue (ha!) I ask Maris, "Do you think blue is a soothing color?" I'm thinking of the blue (cyan) of my swell room, the blue (periwinkle) of the lobster folder, the blue (lapis) of the bay at twilight. "Do you think it's the essence of air and light?"

Never missing an opportunity to swing the spotlight toward herself, Maris says, "I had the talent to be a real painter, not a paint chip painter."

Wake up and smell the Prozac. Wine + Bills = Dreams Overdue.

"Well, not important now," she starts, tracing a circle around her glass with her perfectly mauve nail. "When I was in my twenties in New York, I spent six months producing a series of canvases, wonderful oils of pigs. Sold them to a folk art gallery downtown. Simon and I met at the opening. He loved my work."

Much of this is familiar, but not the farm animals. I interrupt with "Pigs? Where were there city swine?"

Could that explain, even obliquely, the *Charlotte's Web* thread? I turn the faucet all the way to hot and fill the roaster with scalding water.

"Patience," she spits. She looks old when she's mad. Her mouth turns narrow, and the little lines by her chin, nearly invisible most of the time, suddenly seem deep and forever. Most of the time I don't mind having a beautiful mother, but it's also beautiful to see her mortal once in a while.

"Those were the disco days, unfortunately. Afterward, we went to a club, but neither of us were club people. 'Why PIGS?' he screamed. It was very loud. I answered, 'I don't like COWS.'" So lookie there. Maris once had a sense of humor, and it didn't hurt anybody.

"Okay, don't have a cow," I say, proud of myself. My hands are red-raw from scrubbing.

"Cows are cliché." She swings her stocking foot in my direction so I won't miss the dig. "And that was that. He tore his bar napkin in half and scribbled his number on one side. I called him the next day, and we shared a spinach salad and moved in together. Then the folk gallery went belly-up, and we came to Maine, and I enrolled in law school because I couldn't think of what else to do. All in about nine months."

Think: the gestation time for a how-did-I-get-here life.

"Oh, and we got pregnant with you. I forgot that part."

I feel small, anesthetized. Unborn.

The plates stand tall and tidy in the drainer, the kitchen gleams clean. I take a seat next to Maris—possibly to remind her of the outcome of that early love. I cross my legs at the knee and again at the ankle, a pretzel maneuver to keep the shakes at bay, even though, as yet, I don't feel anything threatening my nerves.

I should take this moment to plumb Dad's past, but no single question comes to mind. Instead, I flip through the catalogs on the table, tear out a page of patio furniture—made for people who live in normal houses with normal weather—and fold it into a perfect square. Fold, flip, fold, I'm in the midst of making a paper origami crane. Random.

Or not. An ancient Japanese fable promises to grant a wish for every one thousand cranes folded. I make three. Nine hundred and ninety-seven to go until wish fulfillment.

As a private joke I make all folds with my middle finger. While I am folding birds, I am also flipping Mom the bird. I make two more screw-you cranes and then it occurs to me: The fable says something about folding for others. It's supposed to be an act of generosity.

Maris, perhaps the earth's most ungenerous soul, gets up from the table and pours herself another glass of Pinot. Dad is in his office having Scrabble sex with Lola the laptop.

It's the proverbial fork in the yellow wood/road. I could stay and force myself to think of a question for wine-rambling Mom. Or go down the lesser-traveled road, as it were, to Dad, the protagonist. Stay, I decide. Maybe she's on a roll.

And anyway, the point that's utterly lost on that insipid Robert Frost poem is that it doesn't make a fuck-wad of difference which road any of us take. We all end up in the same uninspired place.

"So, Mom, the pigs. Does that explain why you and Dad were so into *Charlotte's Web?*" Fold one edge to meet the other. I decide I will give the thousand to Noah. I will fold for my Noah-man before he slides into my Nowhere Man.

"I've told you how many times before, Charlotte?"

"A hundred." Or a thousand. Fold diagonally, corner to corner.

"It's a matter of charm," she says. "It's charming. You're so unthinkingly logical, you miss the charm. It's a *bon mot*, and a literary one at that."

If she's going to fence, I can parry (Wordly Wise Word!). "Did you ever think about a fourth child?" I ask. "A Wilbur?"

She hands me her glass of wine. For safekeeping? For sipping? My fingers fuse to the globe.

"There was a fourth. Actually, a second. A child between you and Fern. Now that you are sexually active yourself, I think you deserve to know this."

Whoa. Let's detour on the fact Maris thinks I am having sex with Noah, which I am so not close to doing. Well, I'm closer than I was two days ago, but almost doesn't count in this situation. Ew, she thinks it. Ew, she tells me. Ew in the extreme that she'd probably be disappointed I am not. An object lesson in just how impossible it is to please Maris. I gulp a mouthful of wine. It will turn my tongue Easter-egg purple—at least the half that's not Jewish.

"You were young, twoish, and Simon wasn't working much. I was fresh off interviewing for my first summer law job—and, shit, I found out I was pregnant again. Condoms are fallible. You need to know this."

"You don't have to tell me more." Fallible, phallic. I took too big a swig of wine. There is so no more. She shouldn't share. This is too much—the wrong much—about my parents.

I gently pull open the crane's wings and flick it into flight. Takeoff is amazing. That's my favorite part of flying. The lift. That moment the wheels come off the tarmac before I start counting to forty-five and obsessing about crashing.

"Well, you need to understand this piece of family history." The crane careens off the wall and lands upside down on the floor. "Simon and I weren't getting along."

"Then too?" I ask.

Maris flares her nostrils a millimeter. "Well, I made a tough choice, but thank God I *had* a choice. . . ."

Damage assessment: In the last forty-eight hours I've learned Dad's a cheater, possibly a fugitive, and Mom's a baby-sucker. It's not that I'm a moral prig, or pig, for that matter—I've marched in the NARAL rally in Monument Square. But now it seems a gigantic shame to be denied a siblet who was actually close to me in age, who could be my family in a more organic—as in elemental—way. It's her lawyerly logic that allows her to parse a technical failure from a failure of something else, of heart.

I stand up and take my (now) seven paper birds.

"And thank God you have a choice too. Never let anyone take away your choice," she calls after me in a thick voice as I climb and climb the stairs.

Alone in my perfectly blue room, I take out the Aloha-print duffel bag from Beans (it was on close-out, and no wonder). It is cavernous when empty, a ripstop nylon coffin. I'm obviously not ready to pack, but I just want to know: What will I leave with? What will fit?

I'd take the way Noah's hand feels at the hollow of my back. Okay, more pragmatically, the sheer muslin curtains that look like first-aid gauze when you get up close. The collection, if three count as a collection, of almost-antique perfume bottles from the Brooklyn grandmother. Pictures of the siblets in seashell frames. My flannel pillowcase with turnips, circa age seven. See? I'm more fragile than people think. Oh, and the red sarong Noah bought me at the Blue Hill Fair. What's sarong with me anyway?

I would try to leave stuff behind too. That's the genius of moving on—it's ding-dong-ditch time. I'd dump the pilly stars-and-moon comforter. Recycle the stacks and stacks of maggies that fill my brain with how-to trash. Also the ironic laugh that fools people into thinking I am all ice water, no blood. Maybe I'd leave that at home too, if only I could figure out how.

I unzip the Aloha duffel and step in. Not for some asphyxiation experiment. Just to feel contained by something.

The problem with finding out that I'm the forgotten pregnancy and my sib-to-follow was unchosen is this simple: Now I know. That's a little something I'll have to pack with me, no matter where I'm headed.

I close my eyes preemptively, before the tears even have a chance to decide if they want to come out and play.

Four (a)

I wake with a bolt (and a brrrr), still tucked into my giant duffel/coffin and still wearing last night's clothes.

The beacon on the digital lighthouse clock flashes 4:43. I shut my eyes, but instead of drifting back into happy dreamland, I fall into the nightmare of Maris's confessional conversation.

My eyes snap open—4:44. This is a good omen, a palindromic omen. What the fug, I decide, I'll unzip and make the siblets a first-rate breakfast.

I change into sweats and Dad's flannel shirt and patter off to the quiet kitchen. It's cold and shadowy. I switch on the little lamp he clicked off as a wattage-waster on Monday and pour a glass of grapefruit juice, something with bite. Dad won't buy pasteurized juice out of respect for the fruit, so let's just hope we all won't drop dead of salmonella like the kid in California who keeled after drinking Odwalla.

I heart the idea of cooking a nurturing breakfast. The actual cooking is nice too, but it's the idea I'm in love with. Besides, if I feed the siblets cranberry granola one more day they'll bog down (ha!).

In the laundry room, I take Dad's Wicked Wool socks out of the dryer. Hey, it's cold. It's easy—wheeeee—to slide across the smooth pumpkin pine floor.

I glide over to the back door to let Gussy out. I glide back and grab a polka-dot bowl off the shelf, get a whisk, and spinspinspinspinspinspinspin, ballerina-like, holding the whisk gracefully over my head in third position.

It's almost like there's a finger of vodka in the old juice. I'm buzzed on the promise of the morning. Or still slightly buzzed from guzzling Maris's vino last night. Either way works.

Gussy trots back in quickly. I run a dish towel under hot water and wipe the ice clumps off her paws. I hold her warm snout in my hands and pick the morning googlies out of her eyes.

For whatever reason, the *Nutcracker* overture cues up in my head. It's one sticky melody. A million years ago, I pranced in the ballet's prologue at the Portland Civic Center. In times of curtain-rising anticipation, the bright pizzicato strings come flooding back.

What am I anticipating now? One of the following Fs: finishing, as opposed to obsessing over, my applications, due in almost exactly thirty-six hours; facing Noah now that he knows I'm likely to leave him behind; filtering any future confessions Maris may care to share; or ferreting out the exact facts of Dad's radical past (present)? Bing, bing! All the fugging above.

Gussy trots over. Even the dog knows I'm needy. I rub my arms, try to hug myself. My fingers catch on the perfect stitches around the heart on Dad's controversial plaid sleeve. They actually feel cold and prickly today—like surgical stitches. I wish they would self-dissolve like the sutures that held my lip together after Noah slammed me (unintentionally) with a hockey puck when I was nine.

I've been wearing the shirt a lot, getting tangled in it during REM, making it into a nest-pillow, hoping it will help me get under Dad's skin, as it were, hoping I'm a shirt whisperer who can intuit meaning from the tired cotton.

So far all quiet on the flannel front.

I flip on the little radio on the counter to shut myself up. I keep the volume low, just faint white noise to the louder symphony of eggs cracking, flour sifting, knives thumping, butter melting in preparation for a strata, an egg casserole with multiple semimysterious layers.

The floor upstairs groans. Is someone else awake? I turn off the kitchen lamp and slip the strata into the oven in the dark.

Now it's all of five-thirty and—*voilà*—breakfast is served. But my timing is off. I tiptoe to check in on the siblets, and they are asleep. They haven't turned their faces to the light. The unfortunate yellow of their room undulates in the dawn. I will definitely commit to a new hue before I leave.

I settle into the red rocker back in the corner of the kitchen and daydream, or dawndream, about wall color—leaf green perhaps, as in greener pastures—when I'm jolted by the actuality of Maris entering the kitchen. She is all too real.

There goes the sunrise serenity. She helps herself to a bowl of the ubiquitous cranberry granola. Maris crunches through, and it sounds like she's eating the room. She is the least organic human on the island. Still, she's acquired a taste for the oat.

Gussy lifts her head, sees Maris, and sighs back down. Good instinct.

Is Maris giving me the silent treatment, or has she simply (hopefully) run out of things to say? The muscles in her jaw chomp on—the same way they did last night, pulsing with energy, just dying to share all her dirty baby laundry.

I try to break the ice (ha!) by pouring her a glass of ice water from the striped pitcher on the table. I pour one for me too.

"Up early," I say, handing over what I wish, for the second time in twenty minutes, were a vodka cocktail.

She doesn't say "you too" like a normal mother.

"Just getting my things together."

Now that I'm close to her, right on top of her, I see she's already in Maris mode: black pencil skirt, pink blouse, silk scarf, her brown hair pulled into a perfect low ponytail and fastened with a tasteful tortoiseshell barrette.

"Where did you put my prescriptions again?" she asks.

"Out of the reach of Gussy's nose."

"Specifically," she says, looking very narrow. Very sparrow.

I open the pine cupboard where I've stacked her many meds.

She snatches them with both fists. "Take these for a minute."

I hold out Dad's plaid—an outstretched lap—and she dumps in the amber prescription bottles. The bottles roll around, like I'm gathering apples, except not at all. She jerks a few drawers open. "Would it kill Simon to buy one box of Ziplocs?" she asks. Then she looks at my lap. "I've always hated that plaid of your father's."

My mind yells, "Are you certifiable? You've been back at work a few fucking weeks and you're leaving?" My actual question is quieter. "Where are you going?"

I set the bottles on the counter in an anal row, all labels facing away from me.

"New York." She looks momentarily mystified. "Where else?"

If she were me: to a bucolic campus where kids study under the canopy of a two-hundred-year-old oak tree. Where a high percentage of the student body has dog names: Bailey, Tucker, Riley. A shard of cranberry settles into the corner of her mouth. "Do you need help?" I ask.

She takes my box of contraband Cocoa Puffs, rips the cardboard top off, and dumps the cereal into the compost keeper. A few wayward puffs spin around the counter.

"What are you doing?" I say a little louder, a little faster.

"Saving you from the wrath of your father. You are like him, two peas in a pod, or plaid shirt. I'm keeping you from being unfaithful to the environment."

"We are nothing alike." My stomach cartwheels.

"See? I can recycle too. I'm reusing this," she says, stuffing all the meds into the now-empty, choco-dusty plastic bag and tying it shut with a rubberband for spill-proof travel.

"Mom, did I ask too many questions?" Even though it's murky light, I watch her mouth carefully for signs of trembling.

"No," she says. "Charlotte, people don't panic about the past. People panic about the future. Please don't look at my mouth. I haven't found my lipstick yet."

The tag is sticking out of her blouse, but I don't say "Here, let me fix it for you." I can't say it, something that simple.

"I just need you to do me one favor," she says. "You're the only one who will understand."

"Why not?" Truthfully, I think, Why? And not.

"Run me down to the boat. I don't want to have to change into those atrocious snow boots."

It's such a lovely little relief, her fashion-driven request, that it pricks the icy air. It deflates the worry. We both crack up. I help her zip her leather duffel—enough clothing, I'd guess, for a week. It's not like she's bringing the giant wheelie suitcase. Or the Aloha coffin. "Is there a meeting in New York?"

"Yes, I'm sure there will be." That's the perfect Maris answer. Hazy with a side of snotty.

"Do you need to leave a note?" I ask, slipping into rubber clogs. I don't have an urge to be tall, to be a counterfeit height. We are shoulder to shoulder, close as a sideswipe.

"Note? What kind? Suicide? Oh, a note to your father," she says. "I don't have to. He is well aware."

Whatever the fug that means.

Sometime in the four minutes it takes to steer the old van down to the dock and fishtail home, I get an overwhelming desire to read our family's story.

Which is to say the classic that is *Charlotte's Web*. We have countless copies of the literary wonder. Six or seven downstairs alone.

Maris claims the paperback on the kitchen bookshelf was hers as a child, but she's hallucinating. This one clearly states the copyright was renewed in 1980. Sooner or later the siblets will discover her talent for embroidering memories. The way I see it, why not later?

The best line of the book—and the reason I haven't just changed my name: "It is not often that someone comes along who is a true friend and a good writer. Charlotte was both."

But as I skim, I remember this is really Wilbur's story. It's the story of what I've named my aborted sibling. Me, what's my role? To spout big words. And then to leave. Die, actually, but let's not get morbid.

There's something people don't know about old E. B. White. Elwyn Brooks came to Maine to write children's books after a nervous breakdown, but he was a New Yorker at heart.

You might remember that the first word Charlotte the spider utters is *salutations*. Well, Elwyn preferred to give his salutations, his greetings, to Manhattan, and who can blame him? Certainly not Maris, who is winging to the Upper East Side as we speak.

Last spring, we all took a Sunday drive up to Brooklin, not *that* Brooklyn, but White's Brooklin (Maine also has a Mexico, Sweden, Poland . . . makes me sound well traveled). We came upon E.B.'s son's wooden-boat-building business. Someone in the family figured out how to make Maine work.

The parents should have named me Elwyn. Then I could use his leaving as precedent when I fly the coop or, rather, the island.

With my knees drawn up to my chest at my seat at the table, I'm deep into page eighty-seven when Dad, the only remaining parent, shuffles into the kitchen. He's wearing flannel too. Beans would be proud. He pulls the glass carafe out of the coffeemaker and fills it with water.

I keep reading. The coffeemaker burps to life. Dad swivels my chair around so I'm facing him. My leg goes percussive. He calms my left knee with his warm hand and lands on the hem of the flannel shirt. What will he say about said shirt? Even if he's too bleary to see, he can't help but feel.

"Looks good on you." That's what he comes out with.

"You need glasses," I say, not making eye contact with Dad's profoundly blue eyes.

"You look warm. And the socks too. Full Dad gear."

"Spaz down. It's not some colossal tribute. It's not like I'd leave the house in this," I say, looking up from under my slowly growing-out bangs.

"Liar," he says. "You just drove Mom. What were you trying to do, disarm me?"

Isn't that telling, his choice of words? "What kind of arms do you carry?"

"Long ones." He laughs his raucous laugh, swinging his orangutan arms around. "You know, I was wearing that shirt the first time you saw snow. You held out your chubby fists, to try to catch it."

"And I didn't, right?"

"You caught your share."

He threads his pinky into a buttonhole and pulls me to my feet. The molecules in the air change ever so slightly. Ice on the window crystallizes into a fuzzy snowflake. For a flash I think of Dad's Scrabble board, how everything spiders out from the center like an agglomeration (Wordly Wise Word!) of snow branches.

"You wouldn't go back inside," he says. "Cried if I even took a step. You wanted to stay in the snow forever. In that red-checked snowsuit."

"Eb wears it now," I say.

"A good day. I wrote the date on that puffy snowsuit so I'd remember."

"Sure," I snap. "With invisible ink." I am in no mood for sentimental shit. Just a few months later, he and Mom would abort my little brother. Really, how happy could those days be?

"There is evidence to the contrary. I used a Sharpie. Go look, Debbie Doubter."

I do. I get up and slide to the mudroom and pull the now-faded red gingham off the peg rack. Nada.

"It's on the leg. Close to the cuff."

And damn if it isn't right there under my cold nose. I've steered the shins of Fern and then Eb into this snowsuit for years, but I never noticed Dad's perfectly tiny print: *December 1 . . . 1 P.M.*

"You loved that thing. Loved being out. You were cozy, and I was freezing. Finally you fell asleep. When I took you back inside, my shirt was stiff and my fleece was frozen. I was fleeced."

Despite all that Scrabble, he doesn't play with words as well as I do. Still, maybe I was wrong about the shirt, the Pale Chick, the mystery pix, the mystifying calls, the whole weird chimichanga.

I stand at the sink, hugging the stupid snowsuit. My eyes dart out the window, where I suddenly have a vision of the FBI circling in kayaks. Dad's behind me. For some reason, I do a trust fall, like we all learned to do at the spiritless Sophomore Honors retreat. I surrender.

And what does the fugitive do? First he catches me. Then I feel his hands at my neck. I think, Are these the hands that have wired a bomb (or touched women who are live wires, like Berjan and Kat)?

"Don't move," he says.

I don't. I freeze in place while he braids my hair into one long rope. Maris is feral when it comes to hair. If I ever needed a ballet-bunhead or somewhat-aligned pigtails, Dad was my stylist.

"Do you have a hair tie?"

I do, as always, on my wrist. Susannah calls it my fuck bracelet and tells me I won't wear it once I sleep with Noah. Not likely now. I'll wear it until I leave—or longer.

"Your hair is so you." He gives me a kiss on the eyebrow. "Why don't we eat whatever you cooked up before it's cold? Before it's colder."

"Nice job," I say, fingering the braid.

"It's a challah braid. I went through a challah phase when you were little."

Who knew that either?

I set the table with dish-towel napkins. He steams milk so we can have real café au lait with certified fair-trade beans. Sitting across from each other, in our usual spots, it's a bizarrely normal meal.

"Char, what do you want for the Solstice?" he says between bites, his fork in midair, pointing my way. "What do you really want?"

"I want you to shave. The beard, Dad. It's sketchy."

He strokes the bush he's been grooming for three years. "What if I shave half—the left half? As an experiment."

"Everything you do is on the left," I say. "If it's a present, I choose. All."

"Maybe you won't like me clean-shaven as much as you think."

"Maybe I'd like to see what's under there. Maybe I'll like you more."

Four (b)

Brunswick Day, *Falmouth Pines, Pond Cove, Small World, Topsham . . .*

The school closings purr by in that modulated NPR voice as I get ready to rustle the sibs awake. Small World is shuttered, but Bayside High is arms wide open. Go figure. I listen to the alphabetical recitation twice, just to be sure.

Dad offers to stay home and watch the littles. Maybe he's just trying to notch a Good Dad Day to offset his very long list of Maris-anointed faults. Maybe he will call Maris to gloat when she lands in New York.

Then again, maybe he just wants to have Berjan over for a private yoga playgroup. Downward-facing dog! I still don't really know with Dad.

So it is that for the first time in moons, I am on the Bleak morning ferry solo. I have no stroller gaining momentum down front, no mittens to clip, toggles to toggle, noses to swipe. This is what it would be like to be on my own, still and quiet. I inhale, wanting to fill my lungs with calm. But the air is impenetrable—it may look tranquil, but those snow atoms are jam-packing together. It's a plot to remind me not to take the basics—noses, breathing—for granted.

One silver lining. It's Henry's ferry. Otherwise I wouldn't talk (out loud) to a soul. Only the lawyers who actually show up for work are onboard, plus mutant-perfect Lucia Wood, who has never (never!) missed a day of school.

Henry hands me his coffee with his fuzzy glove. "Drink up. You look arctic."

I take the cup and see concentric circles in the liquid—a bull's-eye.

"Not cold at all," I say, wanting to seem hearty. With my free hand I take off my hat, a twisted act of passive insubordination.

Besides, the maggies say a cold-water rinse makes hair shine—something about molecules shrinking so they lie flat and smooth. This is extreme conditioning.

I take a long draw of his deeply satisfying roast. I wonder which side of the cup his lips sipped.

The heart-attack-inducing air horn blows. We chop off into the chop, and I decide not to go down with the cars but to actually go up to the fresh air, to the tourist spot. Not like it matters, since no tourist in her right (or left) mind would be on the boat this morning.

I bend my knees for balance—I had the sense to wear mid-high heels today (square-toed Mary Janes in red). The warm swallows of the coffee help anchor me. We sleigh-ride down the swells.

I'd guess a ten-foot surge, but then I'd probably be wrong.

I'm not a real Mainer. Our family doesn't have eight generations in the grave. I can't tell the direction of the wind from the way it rattles my cavities, and I can't bake a berry pie without cracking a book. I'm a good cook, but I'm a fraud. I need a recipe, a road map.

Face it: I'm one degree of separation removed from the dreaded rental folk, the people who "summer" on the island, as if a season could be a verb. Two Augusts in the same cottage and they think they invented the headland, the lighthouse, the lobster roll.

Henry staggers back to where I'm now hugging the rail. Mortals would go down below to escape the pitch and spit of the water, but I stay up. I keep an eye on the horizon. He takes his coffee mug back. His eyes are a very deep, almost black, blue. At this moment, everything about him seems solid—thick hair, a steady mood, a habit of openly smiling right into me.

Useless knowledge: Water is eight hundred times denser than air and yet boats float because they displace said water. Useless corollary: One little hole can allow water to get on board and screw with the buoyancy. One little hole can sink you fast.

Henry is so close I can sniff his fennel toothpaste. And that's when I notice a weirdity: His big brown gloves are holding a dainty pink pastry box.

"Special delivery." He leans in and gives me a brush of a kiss on my frozen cheek.

"Say again?" I say, hoping he'll lean again. It's hard to hear over the throbbing of the engines and/or the thrushing of my blood. He smells not at all fishy.

"Happy anything."

"My birthday was two months ago."

"It's for no reason. Just something I've had for you."

"For how long? Is this old?"

"Nah," he laughs. "I've been buying an extra. I've been eating two. But today I took Noah and Susannah over on the first boat." He hands it over.

I open the ears of the box and peer in.

"It's pumpkin," he says. "Almost counts as breakfast."

I take off my striped mitten and swipe my pinkie across the cream cheese frosting. "You have good taste." I glom onto the memory of Noah helping me frost Fern's birthday cake, licking icing from a shared spoon. "Of course, Noah does too."

"Chaunce is trying to organize caroling on the boat this year. You in?" Henry asks.

"Do I look like the type of person who sings songs of joy?"

"You're hard to be nice to."

"Sorry." I don't want to bite the hand that feeds me. The engine surges for a beat or two. Being wordless, so easy with Noah, is hard work with Henry.

"Do you have Trina Schmidt for trig?" he asks. Aside from his monkey ears, he definitely earns his Hunky Henry nickname.

I nod. "Evil troll."

"She's circular. You could turn her on her side at the top of Munjoy Hill and she'd roll right downtown."

That's a conversational cul-de-sac. Try again. Rinse and repeat.

I've been with Noah so long—we ate Play-Doh together at Small World—that I have no innate ability to flirt. Henry is an acquaintance, a practice stranger— as exciting and awkward and unnerving as those preps I'll soon be sharing my morning rituals with.

"How's the lobster season going?" I lob into the dead quiet. What is it with sounding like a grandmother?

Okay, non sequitur, but I just had a lightbulb: I can call her, the grandmother, about my father, her son. She is a bloodline hotline, a DNA descendant. One Passover a few years back, she spent a goodly part of the cocktail hour giving me a guided tour through the family albums. She will remember the shirt. She will remember the Pale Chick in the pix. She will unlock the helix that is my father.

"You ask me a question, then you go mute," Henry says.

"Right. Lobsters."

"It's actually scallop season."

I try to run my hands through my hair, but it's crunchy from the ice. "Oh."

"Scalloping isn't hard. Use the same boat—but you just drag."

"Do you ever want to do something . . . legitimate? Something that doesn't involve living near water? Something that doesn't involve wearing fleece?" What? What am I trying to land on? "Weren't you a Lobster Scholar?" I finally ask.

"Yes, but that's not a job—being a scholar." He picks a piece of lint off my elbow. "People assume I'm a bumblefuck fisherman. That I'm not using my skills. That Yale forklift that sits on the dock in Portland, I use it to load cases of Heineken for islanders who throw big summer parties. That's as close as I'll get to Ivy for a while. College will wait."

"The island will wait too. Where is it going?" Where is this thread going? I was just trying not to be a bitch.

It's Dad who is too fleecy, of course. And Maris who isn't fleecy enough. I have a flicker of watching Maris walk into the sea in her best suit. We know she can swim—if she wants to come back to shore.

"What's a Lobster Scholar anyway?" I ask, even though I know it means a free ride to any Maine college. "Someone who knows lobster trivia? Like the bizarre fact that lobster blood is clear?"

"You're being condescending." He looks right at me.

That shuts me up. "It's a bad habit."

"You'd have a shot at winning. If you stayed."

This is a little bombshell, that he's on to me. "And you know this because . . ."

"Noah. He's a talker."

"So what else do you know about lobsters?" I ask, wanting both to change the subject and pretend to be less bitter. Perhaps even *be* less bitter. "Have you ever seen a blue lobster? Aren't they one in a million?"

"One in two million. There was one on display at the children's museum. Chilly Willy."

"You're not kidding."

"No. I'm actually not funny. The blue lobster is a mutant brown lobster. And when, or if, you were to cook one, it would turn orange, like any other lobster."

"No blue plate special?"

"See? Not funny. We dock in three." He taps

my nose with his glove like I just guessed correctly in charades. "Better get back to my underachieving post."

I look out at the bay expecting to be in the same place—forgetting, for a second, that boats don't stay still. The squat skyline of Portland rises before me. And makes me wonder, What's rising beneath? Is there an odd blue lobster swimming under as we motor on? It could be a one-in-two-million moment completely undetected by clueless me.

For perspective, or for retrospective, I look back to the island and view the view. There's a ruffle of wave licking the halfway-home buoy. Like a ruffle of Henry's hair in a gust.

A beard of fog blurs the details up-island, but the stuff on the coast leaps out. Especially the silhouettes of summer cottages, "cottage" being a relative term since most have, like, seven bedrooms.

I look for the Where's Waldo of our house, a true and honest cottage. I spot its red shingles. I imagine the house is one of those architect's models where the roof lifts right off. I peek inside and see the siblets eating a second breakfast (Dad whisked up some flaxseed pancakes, no doubt). Then the ferry pitches toward the terminal, and I lose my place again.

My toes are Siberian. Even with thick wool socks, party shoes were a crack idea.

The ferry clangs into the slip and Henry takes off his glove—it's whiskered near the thumb from hauling the ropes. He holds out his bare hand. I could use a little steadying. The other guy—Chaunce of the tedious Christmas cheer—helps the few irrational commuters.

"So, happy anything on land too." He leans over for an instant replay of that kiss-but-not-a-kiss move. I suddenly love redundancy. I love that most airplanes have two engines. If one dies in midair, the plane can still fly.

In the falling snow I see a bleary image—someone kneeling, someone come to meet me? Then I laugh at myself. "Is that a seal?" I point my whole mitten in the vague direction of a harbor seal skittering around the dock. The seal's coat looks smooth; new evidence to support the cold-water-rinse theory.

"Yup."

"New?"

"There every morning. Marked its territory. It's not going to leave."

"I'm not leaving quite yet either," I say. The combination of cold toes and warm hands and rich frosting conspire, and I add, "The Solstice Festival is tomorrow night."

"I'll be there."

"Susannah just may be our next Lobster Goddess, our Crustacean Consort," I say.

"There's that patronizing tone again. You've got to work on that."

"I will." I will work to be a bigger person once I'm in a bigger place. Besides, if I become bigger within, perhaps I will become taller without. I could give my feet a break.

Henry stares out to sea, to seal. He plunges his fists into his fuzzy anorak and pulls out some oyster crackers. He heaves them into the water. Gulls swirl and dive, putting on a show, giving him clear positive feedback.

"I will try," I say again because I realize I really mean it, shoes or no.

He opens his fist and hands me a business card— DAVENSPORT IN THE PORT. "Call me when you're hungry," he says. Then he pops an oyster cracker gently, gently into my mouth. Crispy, salty, habit-forming. Yum.

Four (c)

Ms. Schmidt—aka the evil troll trig teacher—is on a tangent (ha!) about cosines and symmetry. There are only four people in class, and that counts Pothead Pablo, who's snoring. Kids who live within snowball-spitting distance of school stayed home today, but not me. I'm like some fugging postal worker. Neither rain nor snow nor gloom of boyfriend will impede my efforts to be a schoolie-doobie.

Though Henry said Noah made the early ferry, he's not in class.

Oh, and where is Oh, Susannah?

I don't see them—separately or collectively—in the cafeteria. Lunch menu: Tofu Teriyaki Bites. Bites is right. Staring into the chasms of tofu on my tray, I think of Henry and his delicate oyster crackers. Maybe we will end up together and open a four-star restaurant. He'll drag the scallops; I'll beat the crème fraîche. He'll trap the lobsters (no goddesses allowed); I'll cultivate the heirloom tomatoes. Together, we'll create food with roots.

The cafeteria is nearly uninhabited. The skinny gray plastic tables in the center, the popularity nucleus, are empty. A few stray girls orbit the edge of the room, near the not-soda machine. Do they even go here? Are they freshmen? They dress in sorbet shades of Abercrombie and Bitch. Like they winter in Palm Beach (see, I can use seasons as verbs too).

This is what it would be like to be the new kid. I would be them. Mental bookmark: dress in achromatic colors so as not to be mistaken for sorbet.

I can't take the pastels anymore—too much like Mom's medicinal palette—so I heel-toe, heel-toe over to the vending machine to junk up. I try to coerce the machine into accepting my crinkled dollar bill. Behind me in line is the mutantly perfect Lucia, island friend of ages ago.

"Do you recall your ninth birthday?" Lucia asks. I look at her blankly. "It snowed," she adds.

The b-day had slipped my mind, but now it comes flooding—well, flaking—back. We were great friends then, before Lucia got so obsessed about getting into Dartmouth—every quiz, every activity, calculated to improve her odds. Like fencing. *Touché!*

"Snowed twenty inches. We all had to sleep over. Think this is a redux?"

Yeah, she uses ten-dollar words too.

I play back the day, a fairy party. I was ridiculously into fairies. At nine I made elaborate houses out of roots and bark and shells and stones. When the snow fell, I asked the whole party to traipse outside to see how the fairies fared during a squall. Lucia stayed out there with me while everyone else wandered back to sip cocoa. The truth is, I was still making fairy villages at age twelve, alone, long after everyone else had moved on to karaoke. The double truth is I was making them at age fifteen too.

Every now and then—more now than then—I try to get Fern to indulge in fairy fantasies, but it's not her idea of fun and games. She is not me.

"We made wings out of cardboard and feathers, remember that?" Lucia asks. This is more than we've spoken in five years. Snow brings out some kind of latent sentimentality in me. Or her. Or both. "Mine were purple. It was a purple phase."

"Right! Mine were mossy." The machine takes my dollar and spits out a Twix.

"Want to sled?" Lucia asks, sliding her quarters down the machine's mouth. Out pops Doublemint gum. Double the pleasure, double the fun.

She offers me a stick. "Why-why not-not?" I answer.

We grab two lunch trays, aka sleds. Most of the old multi-colored trays in the cafeteria were swapped for navy blue (money that would have been better spent, in my opinion, on painting the cinder-block walls a color outside the bruise collection). The old trays, in all their scratched glory, are the sled of choice today. Yay for them.

I hand a lilac rectangle to Lucia, the girl formerly in love with purple. I take an orange.

At the top of the lawn outside the media center, we two-two stand-stand in our respective Penobscot parkas and survey the slope.

It's all downhill from here.

If Ms. Schmidt, the evil troll bitch, were let loose on this hill, she'd tube right into the bay. I imagine Henry discovering her, spouting what turns out to be floating theorems. Or is it me? Is he rescuing me, in search of a theorem I can't actually prove?

The air is deliciously cold. It's a frozen margarita.

Make that a virgin margarita because, really, what I think more than anything is: Wow. This is what it's like to be a little—not a big who simply takes care of a little.

I tuck my considerable hair down into my collar and zip the parka all the way up. Don the hat, don the gay apparel. Lucia has wandered off to assess the knoll by the stoner parking lot. Easy snow, easy go.

Okay. It's time to feel the wheeee!

The first run down is speculative. I zig and zag. I am orange rickrack on a dotted-swiss hill. A caf tray doesn't go so very fast. Still, I slow down in the slight valley before the soccer field, and the packed snow springs up and holds me in its arms.

I use my Icelandic mitty to brush the snow off my ass and rereveal the toes of my red shoes. My jeans are still relatively dry so I trek back. Rinse and repeat.

This time I lie back and surrender to the white stuff. I fold my arms in—look, Ma, no hands.

I'm five, I'm six. Any age short of sixteen.

I throw my weight to my left hip to swoosh over a bump—a stump, a stair, it's hard to tell what's buried beneath.

When I ease to the bottom of the hill, the ride is suddenly and abruptly and forever over.

Because:

Quite clearly I see Noah and Susannah playing a fine winter game of tonsil hockey at the base of the gentle slope, his hand at the curve of her back, her head tilted up to him, her bangs sexy-heavy over her eyes, the whole intersection of their forms at a fuck-me angle. Incredibly bad geometry.

I let out a screak, almost like a burp. I clamp my mitten over my mouth, forcing myself not to add "Excuse me." But it's too late.

The new couple uncouples. They'd heard me.

"Are you okay?" Noah asks. He walks over to my tray and crouches down like he feels sorry for me. Like I'm a little.

"No." I stay on the tray, in a puddle of plastic with my snowy red shoes out in front of me. Not the ice queen but the ice idiot.

"Are you okay?" Apparently he has only one question. He starts to put his arm around me on reflex, then changes his mind.

"I'm a moron." I wonder if this is their first kiss.

"We were going to tell you later today, but it can't be a huge shockeroo," Susannah says. She's glued to the kissing tree. "Noah told me your plans, Charlotte. Shit, boarding school. You're halfway out the door. He's got to move on."

It enters—then exits—my earflaps that I was just having sextracurricular thoughts of my own.

I zero in on Susannah's mouth. She's a lipstick wearer. The two of us would meticulously apply her mother's lipstick, a Revlon shade called Cherries in the Snow (ha!)— a perfect red, not-too-blue, not-too-orange—to each other's mouths when we were ten, in the post-Lucia period.

Maggie tip: To reveal your true face shape, trace the outline of your face in a mirror with red lipstick. Susannah is definitely a heart; I'm a plain old oval. I used to draw and redraw my outline, hoping for some other me to emerge from the glass.

Now Susannah leans her long self over Noah's shoulder. Her bangs touch his collar. I have the urge to chop-chop Susannah's bangs short-short but there are no scissors. So I cut into a scoop of snow with my mitties, and pack-pack it down.

The wool is soaked. Cold hands = cold heart. I smell like a wet dog. I'd give anything to throw my arms around Gussy, to have her fuzzy snout nuzzle the bend of my neck.

The ball takes shape. Pack, rotate, pack, rotate, pack, rotate. Practical physics: Increased pressure lowers the freezing point. I spit on the sphere.

Noah just watches. He's not going to stop me. He's the one who taught me key freeze-o-matic tips like the power of saliva.

I stand and pull my arm back for the release. Susannah backs up. Noah takes a stick and traces a peace sign in the snow. It's possible that I am melting, the ice idiot in deep thaw. It's hard to tell if my eyes are simply stinging or if my tears have betrayed me and are open for business.

Whack. I throw the snowball into the ground. It breaks apart. I pack and throw another. And another.

I know where the white goes when snow melts. Regular old water is clear because all its molecules are perfectly aligned, very anal-like, very me-like. Not so snow. Snow is random. It's made up of these irregular drops. Our eyes see all that chaos as white. And when the chaos melts away, snow turns transparent and crystal clear.

While I'm off on my snow trance, Noah walks to my side. Susannah is nowhere visible. He scoops a little pile of his own snow. "Look, it wasn't planned. It definitely wasn't planned by me. I'm sorry."

"I get it," I say, kicking my ridiculous shiny red shoes into the ground, flinging snow everywhere. I get that Noah is history. That my apps are all but complete. That Dad is flawed in some deep, potentially disturbing way. That Mom is on the lam. And that I will soon leave too/two.

"This is the first time. The first day, anyway."

"I don't care." I can't look at him. I look at his shadow.

The shadow moves nearer, larger. His actual self isn't close because I can't smell him. But his outline swallows me. "Exactly. You don't care at all. You made it pretty clear how much you care about me." He snuffles, like Gussy—freezing or tearing up, I'm not sure.

My new favorite person, Lucia, shows up with someone's bright yellow inner tube around her neck, a giant neon lifesaver (ha!).

"Sorry to steal her, Noah," she says. "But, Charlotte, you have got to try this."

"Yes, I do," I almost scream, my head tilted skyward to catch the falling flakes. "I have to try it."

Four (d)

I drop Lucia at AP Econ, find out *Français* is cancelled, and head to the media center alone. I set myself up with my lobster folder at one of the ridiculously unreliable computers. I swivel the screen around and sit on the edge of my chair so I can see the door.

Just in case I have a visitor or, worse, two.

Short and vivid. That's what I'm after. It's tough to write applications when I'm out of my element. No soundtrack—no Clash, no Rufus. No glass of water, no unpasteurized juice. No wood desk under the eaves of my absolutely blue attic. Definitely no "*CHARLOTTE ♡ NOAH*" scratched in the pine.

In an attempt to make the media center more convivial (Wordly Wise Word!), I arrange a few number two pencils, my lucky purple pen, and a fluorescent pink highlighter in an empty Nalgene bottle. Ta da, a little school-supply bouquet.

The highlighter highlights (ha!) my memories of last summer, the beginning, now that I think of it, of my wanderlust. I'd grab the classifieds, rev the primordial van and scout with a laminated island map. I'd stick little pink dots over houses for rent/sale I liked better than our own. Those with golden families to match the light that bled from every pane of their many-paned windows.

If Fern were with me, she'd try to connect the dots. "A whale?" she'd guess. "An eggplant?" By Labor Day my longing was out of control. The pink had metastasized. What it really added up to was a whole lot of pining (and not the Great Northern variety) for another life.

Breathe. Two questions left, and I'm avoiding one (the dreaded "What do you like best about yourself?").

So. Short-answer question two.

WHO IS YOUR FAVORITE LITERARY CHARACTER?

Sloppy copy:

I could say Catcher in the Rye*'s Holden because what sophomore doesn't love ironic detachment— that and the fact he ditched boarding school, the type I'm trying to charm a spot into. I could also pick Yossarian of* Catch-22 *because I too care about the paradox of war.*

But as Mr. Trice would say, Write what you know. So je m'appelle Charlotte. My sibs and I (my sibs and moi?) were named for characters in

Charlotte's Web, *the State of Maine's valentine to children's lit.*

What's in a name anyway, as the Bard might ask. Name your price, name that tune, in the name of God. Nickname, brand name, nom de plume. *At least I'm named for the protagonist. At least I'm not Templeton, the rat.*

There are other literary Charlottes. Brontë (auteur *of* Jane Eyre). *Perkins Gilmore* (auteur *of* The Yellow Wallpaper, *a short story I appreciate for its decorating subtext). Something by Goethe, which I should know. In French,* Charlotte *means* petite. *I am so true to my name, in fact, that femur implants figure regularly into my fantasy. Until Susannah knocks into my fantasy and it falls on its ass.* Susannah *must mean* grande *in an unspecified language because she has criminally long femurs, among other perfections. Susannah should be named Templeton, for the fucking rat.*

I clap my palm over my mouth, afraid I said "fucking rat" aloud. No, I decide, it's just the lousy keyboard clacking in my ears.

The fascination with words, with letters, which are the ABC's of words, as my preschool teacher Berjan would say, is genetic. She may be shtupping my father. Shtupping is one of those kinder-Yiddish words I referred to in question three. It means to fuck. My shtupping father is in love with letters. Words seem too big a commitment for him, but he is all over letters. His highest Scrabble score is 657, which, on a relative basis, is more impressive than my perfect PSAT score. Perhaps he should apply to your school. Perhaps he should leave the island, not me. It seems my mother has already sailed away.

Maybe this is the time to mention that I excel at calculus, but not at literary progression. As Mr. Trice says all the time, I'm overjumping the story.

Compare: *Ways that Charlotte A. Cavatica, the spider, and Charlotte A. (for Alice) Wise, the applicant, are alike:*
Nearsighted
Love words
Care about design
Weakness for punctuation (some pig!)
Enjoy the ritual of food preparation
Not instantly likable
Like to hang out under the eaves
Contrast:
Charlotte Cavatica drinks blood
Charlotte Cavatica stands on her head for profound thoughts

I take a break and decide to give the headstand trick a go. Noah and I used to do yoga with the preschool teacher Berjan. It is a Small World, after all. Why not try life from Charlotte the spider's view?

I walk over to Dewey decimal 716 (herbaceous plants) and kick off my still-wet red shoes. I kneel and place my head a few inches from the unthinkably blue-gray wall. I intend to keep the ski cap on, but when I become one (om!) with the linoleum, the pom-pom sinks into my scalp. Without the hat, I'm sure I have attractive hat-hair.

And the itsy-bitsy spider climbs up the library wall. Shit. Down come the legs and the itsy-bitsy spider climbs back to the desk again.

Back to sloppy copy:

Aside from chugging blood, oh, and also hairy legs (I'm not so French-obsessed as to go au naturel with the leg hair), we are interconnected. I hope to learn from Charlotte how to leave others. I assume I won't die to make this point. Charlotte didn't really die for Wilbur, by the way. People interpret her actions as powerful maternal sacrifice. Please. Her death was inevitable. At some point, it is time to go.

Charlotte and I also share a love of animals. I'm devoted to my dog, some poodle. I will miss her whines and nudges. I will miss looking for the errant pink tuft of fur on her front right paw. It's hard to imagine sharing the world without a licky beast—or without sticky children. Can I bring my dog? My kids? They're no bigger than a poodle.

Here's my final observation. If I were religious, and I may be, I'd say the Shehecheyanu prayer now. It's only eleven words. Our rabbi, who drinks like a fish (not like a lobster, because that wouldn't be kosher), encourages me to say it whenever I feel unique in this world. E. B. White is rumored to have been an anti-Semite. I can live with that because, ultimately, I want to be my own person, not some anthropomorphized version of a legend. Besides, Joe Walsh, he of the legendary guitar lick, says, "You can't be a legend in your parents' basement." Or attic, for that matter.

Spell-check wants me to change *rabbi* to *rabbit*. Fuck you, Microsoft Word.

Short and vivid was the goal. I'm long and off point. I head (ha!) back to the plant tomes for a headstand stint.

I kick and stay up on the first try. Gravity inverted, I shift my eyes around.

Outside, the snow is falling upside down. The ground is the sky, and it is covered with white fluffy clouds. I check the door in case Noah appears to turn my world right side up. He doesn't. I stay capsized until the blood drills down into my head. Despite my best intentions, I tip over.

Four (e)

The aptly named Ms. Bloch, a square-faced guidance counselor, takes the note I've flawlessly forged granting me permission to pick up my transcript to include with my due-in-twenty-six-hours applications.

Sealed envelope in hand, I smack into Lucia in the dusky hallway. "What are you going to do?"

I scrunch my forehead.

"No ferries," says Lucia. "The winds, they're wicked."

Although I vowed never to say the *w* word, I let Lucia's usage slide, not wanting to insult my only remaining friend. Besides, they must be mighty *w* winds to ground the ferry. I remember the boat being canceled exactly thrice—twice for hurricanes, once for radar failure.

"My dad got a hotel room by the mall. You can bunk with us," Lucia says.

Okay, no can do. Her dad, Lester, is creepy. If Simon is an eight on the one-to-ten weirdness scale,

Lester-the-Molester is a twelve. He wears his under-wear, only his underwear, around the house, even when handing out Halloween candy (ew). Not boxers either.

I borrow Lucia's cell, a snazzy silver number, and pull Henry's card out of my pocket. It's grainy—a little surplus salt from this morning's crackers.

He picks up on the first ring and confirms that Lucia is right (really, why am I surprised?). Gusts are running sixty-five knots, and it's not safe to dock. "Lucky Susannah. She caught the last boat out." Lucky Susannah indeed. "I'll bring you a morning cupcake," he says. I let the pastry possibility hang in the air.

As long as I'm dialing, I check in at home. Fern answers after ten rings.

"Hi, frond," I say. "Having a good snow day?"

"We made a snow fort and iced it over. Dad taught us to hunker down." Figures.

Fern reports that Dad is locked in an online Scrabble marathon with a grandma from Anchorage. Mom has not yet called in, as if it is perfectly normal to have walked out on her family for no apparent reason. See, she leaves without it being a production. Maybe I need to take a page from her brief.

I hear Dad's voice rise in the background. "Hold up. I need to talk to Char," he says.

"Are you winning?"

"Five hundred thirty-one so far. So yes. Listen, you're set. I called Noah's mom. Libby has Noah tonight, as you no doubt know. You can stay with them in Portland."

"Dad, we broke up." To hear myself admit it to someone other than my subconscious is a shock. I chew my tongue. I hold my incisors in place until I can taste the metal tang of blood.

"Well," he says. "Well, my timing is off. As usual." He's silent for a long minute. Tick. So am I. Tick. Then: "I don't see the choice. Listen, you two have been friends forever—before you were more than friends. You can survive one night, one more night under a roof together."

I glance at Lucia, thinking of Lester and his tightie whities. "Right, no choice," I say.

I snap the phone shut and bite the metal. I swab the spit and a small filament of blood with my sweater sleeve and hand it back to Lucia, who doesn't blink. She's kinder than I remember.

Noah is around the corner, leaning back against his locker. He has an underground zit about to surface on his chin. "Mom left a message with the school office. She says you're staying."

"Your zit is talking to me."

"It's saying, 'You can stay with us.' "

Beyond the zit, he looks done in. His eyes are distended like he has a disease. The disease of deceit.

"We can do this," he says, looking a little lost at sea. I nod.

We slip-slide the few blocks to his mom's house. I lead the way so I don't have to stride beside him, but I'm walking without landmarks. The streets are blank. Snow blankets the cars. They're massive marshmallows. If I hadn't seen Noah making out with Oh, Susannah, I'd lace my arm through his and whisper "s'mores" into his cold ear. Instead I interlace my fingers. I hold my own hand.

The red door beckons. I love this house. The tall bookcases. The wood floors as rich as a chocolate bar. The utter lack of clutter. The dog, Otis, a golden retriever who doesn't eat contraband. The mom, an entirely sane architect, who doesn't need meds to begin with, who doesn't need to up her dose.

Noah opens the fridge. In the slanty light he looks glum. "Want something? Applesauce?"

Otis wags over. I take a Coke and walk with Otis to Noah's room. Now that the entire world has tilted, I have to see if his room is reversed, if I am still standing on my head. But no, his room looks remarkably regular. I'm especially proud of the T-shirt curtains. We ran a rod through the armholes of his summer tees and, *voilà*, window treatments, as the maggies say. I scan the camp shirts, past and present. Noah made the tie-dye tee, second from the left, the summer after third grade.

I break out of memory mode when I hear Libby come home. Otis goes in for the greet, but I stay behind. Let Noah deliver the headline that her perfect son is a big fat cheater. Maybe Libby knows already. She's the kind of mom who's always in the loop, the anti-Maris.

I count to forty-five—the magic plane takeoff number. I count again—I need round-trip karma. Then I walk loudly into the kitchen. Libby opens her arms and folds me into her soft sweater in nuanced shades of gray.

Libby *is* her shoes. She wears Birkenstocks, like the rest of Maine, but hers are black patent leather. She fits in with a twist.

"Let's deliver. Thai? Fried clams? You guys choose."

"I can make eggs," I say. My cheeks flush. Crack some eggs. That's how the day started, so promising.

Noah stands about two feet away, flipping through the paper.

"Great. Otis likes eggs," Libby says, giving me a thump on the head. I know she loves my asparagus frittata. "Let me dry you," she says, tugging at my wet jeans. "There are stratiform clouds, which means more snow tonight. Take a nice shower."

Libby knows her weather—and her son. And me.

"Okay," I say. "I'll take a quickie."

I head into Noah's yellow and black bathroom. Bee happy. The floor is freezing. I lie down and press my cheek against the tile. Have I been this hot all day? I spin the water dial to cold and force myself not to yelp for help.

After a nippy shower, I open Noah's medicine cabinet looking for something inculpating (Wordly Wise Word!). But it's just his stuff. His deodorant, his Tylenol, his old retainers in their red plastic case, his condoms.

I open the box and count the Trojans: hup 2, 3, 4. Hup 6, 7, 8. Counting the four we saved for later (two in my wallet, two in his), all are present and accounted for. No soldier AWOL.

I spritz on his bluegrass cologne. Now I have him on me. I didn't think that part through. With the buttery-soft washcloth, I try to slough him off.

Dad's infamous Beans shirt is still in my backpack, and I put it on along with a pair of Noah's boxers I pluck out of the clean laundry basket. I hate him in my head, but my body hasn't caught on—it still wants him against my hot skin.

Back in the kitchen, Libby pours herself a glass of wine and wanders off. Otis follows, leaving Noah and me alone. I grab a straw for my Coke so I'll have something to chew on if I don't feel like talking.

"Frittata?" I ask.

"Fine. And how are you?"

I crack hup 2, 3, 4 eggs into a bowl.

"People think first love is a joke," I say, beating the yolks and turning on the burner, waiting for the tick, tick to click in.

I pinch my wrist. I forgot to slip on a new elastic. Let Susannah think I've slept with him already. The butter hisses in the skillet. In go the diced onions, let them sweat. I pinch again, harder.

Noah walks over and stares in the pan. "How can you plan something and not tell anyone?"

"You mean a frittata?"

"The other thing."

I hold out an olive, a peace offering. "I didn't know how to do it."

He shakes his head, no peace. "You should have told me."

"You wouldn't have gotten it." I put my hands on my hips, on his boxers.

"How do you know? You have both sides of the conversation in your busy head."

I lean in and give him a Henry kiss, a little brush on the cheek. "Are you wishing I caught the last boat and she was here? Are you looking at me and thinking about her?"

"I'm thinking of you. I'm mad at you."

I pop the rejected olive in my mouth. Then I put my hands in his back pockets. It's a push/pull thing. I loathe him (push), and I love him (pull). My busy head balances the two mismatched ideas—so much double-think for one day—and comes down on the side of history, of love. Of pull. Our hipbones kiss. Useless AP Biology knowledge: When horny, twenty extra gallons of blood rush to the pelvis.

"Those of us who are left, we feel unmissed," he says into my wet hair.

What I'll miss. The vanilla cones at Reds, cutting his hair, the hair on his legs, his boxers with me in them, his boxers with him in them, the pesto, the undertow.

The real undertow, the time he jumped in and grabbed a drifting Fern, and the undertow of knowing almost everything there is to know about a single person.

I pull myself into him a little deeper, deep with grat-itude or forgiveness or even, implausibly, emotion.

"Wait," Noah says, pulling back for the third time in four days. "Let me tell you about Susannah. Now that everything is out in the open. Or almost."

I oh-so-casually cover my mouth to control my

reaction, like the whole conversation is one big yawn. "Are we playing truth or dare with only truth?" I say. I sound muffled behind my hand.

He slowly nods. His hair shakes against his shoulders. "We've been together. We've slept together. Actually, we didn't sleep."

"No? No. I counted." Condoms, that's what I mean. The Trojans standing at attention in their unempty box.

"We used hers. She was prepared."

Wow. And also: Wow. I forget to exhale. I need to give myself CPR.

"Where? When?" Now I overcompensate, gulp for air. I purse my lips in a whistle and breathe in and out.

"At her house." Her bland house. Her stain-resistant beige carpet. "And last night. About ten o'clock. Or ten-fifteen. It was the first time. Obviously."

"You said that earlier today when your tongue was down her throat. Obviously it wasn't the first time. Liar. When did you turn into someone I don't know?"

"About ten hours after you did," he says.

Why is the most popular brand of condoms called Trojan anyway, like the Trojan War? That's a sick joke at my expense.

I force my shoulders to relax and ask, quietly, "Didn't the Trojan horse have enemies in its belly? Sound familiar?"

Noah chops the tough ends of the asparagus I discarded. "I'm sorry."

"I thought we'd always be together," I say, getting tears in my eyes. I try to push them back into their ducts, deep into the hallways inside my head, where I've constructed an entire sad house of uncried tears.

The pinging sound may be the breaking of my heart. That and the timer announcing the oven is preheated.

My appetite is MIA, like Susannah's condom. I fixate on Libby sipping her red wine, swirling the goblet by its stem, making waves. Like Charlotte Cavatica, I have a sudden insatiable taste for red. I clear the table and offer to wash the pretty pottery dishes.

I can't see the black and wavy ocean from this kitchen sink like I can at home. Here, the many-paned window just divides my face and reflects it smack back to me—except in pieces. I picture the peak of the waves, the peak of the egg whites.

Here's the thing about peaks, egg and otherwise. There's a moment of perfection, and then it's gone. The peaks go leaden. Or flat. Or forgotten.

"Tired?" Noah asks, grabbing an Eiffel-tower dish towel to help me dry. Libby has the Paris passion too.

"Dog-tired," I answer, petting Otis, who waits optimistically by the sink.

"I'll finish," he says.

I snuzzle with Otis on the sage sofa for a dog nap.

For some time, hours apparently, I doze. In a semi–dream state I hear "wake up."

I open an eye to see Noah sitting next to me, half off the sofa, wearing a fleece and hat. "It's midnight."

My rousing thought: What's with the avocado pit in my stomach? "I remember. I hate you."

"I know. Hate me later. Hate me tomorrow. Tonight, I want to take you somewhere. Somewhere happy."

I'm back to the pull part of push/pull. Who turns down happy? And where are my wet red shoes?

Four (f)

The digital clock beams 12:20 in Noah's mom's Subaru. I buckle up.

"Wait a minute," I say, having a hard time catching my cold breath.

"Want your butt warmer on?" Noah asks.

"Sure." Who wants a frosty ass? The clock changes to 12:21, palindromic luck. "Okay," I say. "Now we can go."

He leans into me and flicks the switch on the side of the seat. He smells like the bluegrass cologne I spritzed on then scrubbed off.

"It's the middle of the night, but it's really tomorrow," he says in a pseudo-cheerful way. The roads are slightly slick but sanded.

Afraid of what will come out of my mouth or my heart, I don't say anything. Instead I root around the glove box for the Ironix Mix CD I made Libby for her birthday: Spin Doctors, Stones, Scaggs, Smashing

Pumpkins. I lean back into him—tit for tat—and feed the disc to the starving CD player and let the music fill us up.

The cautious boy grips the steering wheel in the archetypal ten-and-two-o'-clock position. Outside, the flakes drift down in slow-mo. I am inside a snow globe looking out. Last Solstice I made snow globes as prezzies. It is frightfully easy to fake the shimmery magic of a snowfall. All it takes is a mustard jar, distilled water, glycerin, and a pinch of glitter. Flip and *voilà*. Let it snow.

You think I'd demand to know where my unfaithful boyfriend is taking me. But I know. Without him saying a word, I get it, get him. We're going to Beans. There are others around the country, but those are chiefly outlets—second-bests. Twenty minutes north of Portland is the original, one-and-only flagship, the mothership, the lobstership.

We've been there in daylight a million times, but the midnight run is something we've talked about. All Mainers do—natter on about shopping in the predawn for proof the store is really open 24/7/365. The doors have allegedly been shuttered only twice: when JFK was killed and when Leon Leonwood Bean himself kicked.

Noah skirts the highway and heads up Route 1 past the BFI (Big Fucking Indian), a giganto fiberglass chief who inexplicably showed up near an auto-repair shop one day. We face the chief head-on. A demented part of me wants Noah to slide into the firmly planted Wabanaki just to feel the impact of connecting with something solid. I crank the music to save myself from being crazy out loud.

We fishtail into the Beans parking lot where there is an unheard-of spot smack in front. Three million people walk through these doors in a year, but not tonight. No evil tour buses, no chubsters from Indiana. It's a DMV parking-test paradise.

Sure enough, the lights are ablaze on this snowy night/morning—acres of hand-sewn moccasins and flannel dog beds waiting just for us. I get out of the car and kiss the laces of the two-story-high Maine hunting shoe by the entrance.

Never before have I wished I had a pair of these iconic boots. Prada pumps, Gucci mules—those are the objects of my fondness. Tonight, though, I'm dying to slip my wet toes inside these Thinsulate liners, to be utterly at home in my own two feet.

At the front door, a bored-looking sales associate with black fingernail polish offers us a hot beverage. Coffee or tea? She could be a goth flight attendant. She doesn't fit the Beans mode—she must only come out at night.

I'm dreaming but for real—I wish I could control the ending, the landing, wish I could wake up and reinvent the whole week, the whole flight plan.

I make myself a cup o' cocoa, then one for Noah. It has real marshmallows, like the mounded cars, not like the ossified pencil erasers in the Swiss Miss packs. The Muzak is loud—there are too few customers to absorb the carols.

When in doubt, do shop—that's classic maggie advice. Cleaving to our cocoas, Noah and I head up to the third floor, taking the stairs two at a time. Noah picks up a fishing vest for his dad. A guy with the name tag Chris suggests a hygrometer for the weather-infatuated Libby.

I choose a fuzzy red collar for Gussy and look at Nordic mitties for the siblets, but I suddenly don't know if their hands are extra-small and small, respectively, or small and medium. I sit on a child-size Adirondack chair and scrunch my eyes, trying to conjure the littles. The best I come up with is a composite sketch—teeny nose, long lashes, faint freckles. I haven't even left, and already I can't picture them.

Related and reassuring thought: If I forget faces in only twenty-four hours, surely the FBI would forget details of Dad decades after the fact.

"What about Maris?" Noah asks. "What are you going to get her?"

"Let's skip her," I say. She who skips town. I haven't had time to share with Noah that she's drifted off, what with his busy shtupping schedule.

If/when Mom ever returns, gift in hand, it will be another gold charm for that bracelet I never wear. I have quite the trinket collection: a clown (which I abhor), ballet slippers (though I haven't twirled in tu-tu long), and a filigree heart (a heart with holes!). I always tell her I want a useful prezzie—a pair of nonrusty ice skates or an alarm clock—but she insists on buying hopeless charms.

Her motto: Nothing's irrevocable. It's supposed to be liberating, the idea that you can always return something you don't want. But I'm not a returner, I'm a keeper.

While Noah goes in search of food—sugar, ideally—I head down to the second floor.

Without exactly planning to, I walk my red Mary Janes right into shoes.

You know where this is going.

I must have the suddenly irresistible Beans boots. Funny how I spent eons in opposition. The combination of rubber and leather, the roomy toe box, the chain traction made to traverse island woods—or forests of academia. Even I acknowledge that there are some things Maine does really well.

At the customer service desk, I charge the boots to Maris (her Amex number coming in handy yet again). I park my dampish red shoes in the box and let my feet move and breathe and dance in their new nonheeled home.

Noah waves to me from over by the trout pond. From behind his back he pulls a little Beans boot cast in chocolate. Great minds . . .

The real time is 1:41 A.M.—another palindrome— but inside the store it's fake day-bright. It's always sunny, always noon. Together we sit on a Hatteras hammock, staring at the faux boulders on the rock wall, passing the boot back and forth like a joint. For a good forty minutes we see no other shoppers, just our feet coming up for air, mine looking burnished and warm and new.

"This is nice," he says. "Brings back memories."

"Of who?" The words dart out by mistake. It sounds like I'm fishing. Fishing for a compliment near a pond stocked with baby trout. My brain can't help but replay his encouraging words about my awkward breasts during our last hammock foray. I slap my arms over my chest and compress myself.

"Only you." He bites his top lip when he says it. He doesn't touch me. I mean, he doesn't reach over. Still, I'm a little touched.

I could make a deal with him right here in the middle of the pretend day. I'll stay in Lobsterland; you leave the Lobster Goddess. We'll forget this week and live blithely ever after in our Beans hammock.

"You think we could go back?" I test the waters out loud.

"To what?"

"To together." We swing shoulder to shoulder.

"Pretty complicated," he says. He might be on the edge of crying, but I can't turn my head without accosting his ear.

"We could hit the reboot button. If we wanted to," I say, eyes locked on my new feet. "If we both wanted to."

"This is a game . . . ," he says. *Clap clap.*

"Really? That's what you want to do now?" I ask. But I can't help myself. "Of concentration . . ." *Clap clap.*

"No repeats . . ." He speeds up. *Clap clap.*

"Or hesitations." *Clap clap.*

"I'm going first," he says, dropping the clap. "The category is . . . U. Uncomfortable."

"Unfaithful," I say fast.

"Unfair."

"Unconditional." I kick the fake grass and swoosh us higher.

"Unconditional—no way! Don't lie," he says. "Undecided."

"Underhanded."

"Right back at you. Underhanded."

"Underwear—not mine."

"Undo." He pushes off hard. The shiny hooks that hold the hammock to the half walls yaw.

"Really?" I ask on the upswing. "Undo?"

"Unanswerable," he says. For the first time I can remember, he has the last word. We jump off and let the hammock sway itself silly without us. Unrestrained.

Stretching tall (a relative term), I drift one department over to the camping compound. Real time: 2:22. I crawl into a display tent with a blue-and-gray dome. It's surprisingly roomy inside. I do a small tight somersault.

"Noah, come see," I say, poking my head out the front flap. He's looking at water purification backpacks.

Salesguy Chris could give a hoot. Neither, for that matter, could the taxidermy owl.

Inside the tent, Noah and I face each other. Shafts of artificial daylight seep through the window flaps. Still, it's shadowy enough to be disorienting.

"So I guess we won't live in France together," I say after a few minutes. I remember the fantasy was actually about not-Noah, but never mind.

"You never clued me in on the French fantasy. Who says I would have liked it?" He lies down and props up on one elbow, looking at me. In the twilight dark, I can't make out his eyes.

I stretch out facing him. We are nearly touching everywhere, nose to toes. We're alone, together—close as sex. I can't hear the canned Christmas carols from here. Only the sound of my own deep exhales. It's a riot of quiet.

"What's not to like?" I answer his question of, like, an hour ago. "The Paris fantasy was all about good food and pretty dishes and making out and making love." In this crucial Noah/not-Noah moment, I want to fondue it. Fondue it right now.

He interlaces the tips of his fingers with mine. Melt.

This thawing, liquefying, actually, of my heart unleashes something else. Once the torrent starts, it's hard to stop.

Forget what I said about not obsessing aloud. The cocoon of the tent—and the proximity of my oldest, deepest friend in the universe—conspire to crack me open like a piñata. I sit up, knees akimbo, and face the eyes I can't see.

I start with Mom. The abortion confession. The philanderer declaration. Then on to Dad. The shirt. The TV. The Pale Chick pix. I rattle off questions about Simon/Si: Is he in the witness protection program? Will he come clean and change his socks? Will he adopt a normal hobby that doesn't involve a Scrabble opponent in Juneau? Sorry. Anchorage. These are likely the wrong questions. The right ones are unaskable. Unanswerable.

I come full circle, back to the shirt.

"This shirt?" Noah asks, fingering the patch on my sleeve.

I bobble my head.

"Let's go get him another one."

"It's not made anymore." I checked—up on him.

"Charlotte, we're at Beans. It doesn't get any plaidier."

I crawl out ass-first. It's now 3:15—no palindrome. I grab a shirt for Dad—any plaid will do—because what I'm really itching to do is inch back into the tent.

While I wait for gift wrap, Noah pay-phones home and spills the beans (ha!) to Libby that we'll spend the night in Beans. We aren't the first to do this. It's not an advertised benefit, but plenty of people have camped out (and more, much more) under this steeply angled roof.

Noah says the roads are bad. Libby must sense there's more to the story, but exemplary mom that she is, she must also sense this is a time to be responsibly irresponsible.

I bounce backward, past the various global ecosystems on display, to our home sweet tent. I am a wandering Jew. "Will you read my apps? They're a mess. I'm a mess."

I may have the highest GPA at Bayside, but Noah is two hundredths of a point behind me. He's on my heels.

"They're here?" he asks.

"In my backpack. I started, but I'm going nowhere. Deadline is Friday at five. I guess that's today. In thirteen hours and some-odd minutes."

"I'll look," he says. Noah borrows a tiny but potent high-beam flashlight from the travel section.

On Monday I wanted a flashlight to shine around the edges of my life. And here I am (or he is), flashlight in hand. Somehow the picture does seem a little brighter. Not clearer. There's still a focus issue—the soft-focus of the Unanswerable. Still, bright is a beginning.

I take out the lobster folder with my sloppy copies. Part of me is embarrassed to have Noah see me so naked on the page. But only part. The other part of me, against all logic, wants to get naked with him *off* the page, right here in the ultra-dome display model.

Even though my PSAT-perfect brain understands we are over, it will take time to crush the habit of loving him.

"Okay, this question about personal accomplishment. What about caring for Fern and Eb?" he asks, crinkling his forehead. "Isn't that huge, way more important than a pirouette? If you're going to do this, at least tell the truth about yourself."

I'm silent; he's silent.

"Let's point toward truth," I finally say.

We put our heads together in the dome, editing and reworking four out of five of my essays by the intense light of the halogen beam. I lie on my stomach first. Noah joins me. I throw my clunky new boot over his leg, and he moves closer until there is no air between us. Our exhales synchronize. On our stomachs, feet intertwined, it feels like we're sharing a towel in Saint Tropez. At least that's the way I imagine it.

By 4:30 A.M. we're pretty much *fini*. Noah clicks off the flashlight. In the vague dark, the tent turns claustrophobic. I stretch my neck to one side, then the other, trying to find fresh air.

Balling up my fleece, I lie on my back and stare straight up through the plastic weather-watcher window cut into the ripstop roof. I imagine Cassiopeia is nine inches above my lashes lowering itself into me.

Useless knowledge: Idiots who live in New York have an aborted view—the angle of the tree line slices into their vista. In Maine, latitude forty-five degrees, we see more planets on the horizon. In a way it doesn't matter. I am here but already half gone, already half living in a subpar latitude with a constricted sky.

Noah dozes first. To calm the night jitters, I reflexively slap my palm over my thigh. But, unthinkably, my legs aren't aquiver. No metronome. I give Noah an in-the-dark kiss—fleeting but real. I take his heavy hand and fling it over my heart.

He's warm, I'm warm. Fully dressed, in the middle of a fully open store, we spend our first night together.

FRIDAY

Five (a)

Noah is nowhere to be seen, his hand definitely not on my heart. The light in the store remains unchanged—perpetual high noon—but my watch confirms it is legitimately morning. It's 6:03, aka ten hours and fifty-seven minutes before my applications are due.

I untie the tent flap and find the Noah-man outside the "campground" at a farmhouse table display, cups of coffee from the café at the ready. My purple pen in hand, he's making notes on my getting-better prose.

Oddly he wears a striped scarf with two giganto bouncy pom-poms at the bottom. "For you," he says when I join him in the mock kitchen. "A Solstice gift." He unwinds the scarf from his neck and throws it over mine. It's warm, prewarmed, by his skin.

"What a ball! *Très* testicular," I say, bouncing the pom-poms from side to side.

"These read well now," he says, tapping the pen onto my sloppy copies, speckling the page with purple. He is in gear; he's not falling for my jokes. "You're in good shape."

My mouth tastes brackish. "I'm gonna brush up," I say, even though I don't have a toothbrush.

In the bathroom I lean my palms against the sink counter and stare into the twig mirror. Somehow my freckles have coalesced into a landmass on my cheeks. Instead of individual islands surrounded by fish-belly skin, the dots are huddled. They are gathered to give me strength, perhaps. I wet a paper towel with scalding hot water (maggie tip!) and scrub the overnight plaque off my teeth.

Noah is back on the pay phone when I return, poking the little coin return slot. He hands me the receiver. "Bleak," he whispers.

"We have a snow delay. All of us, actually," Fern says.

"We do, actually?" I ask, mocking her just the tiniest bit. Dad confirms it: a two-hour school delay, but the winds are down, and the ferries are up and running.

This is good news, actually. Factually. It means I have time to head to Bleak. Time to change clothes, dress the kinder, feed the Gussy, and still get back over before the first bell. That and grab the rest of my official b.s. paperwork.

Outside the sky is on a dimmer switch. If it's hundred-watt sunshine inside Beans, it's a limp and flickering bulb here. Simon would be pleased—low energy usage and all. Perhaps the sun is simply petrified.

The Subaru warms quickly—such a considerate car. Bare trees, polished smooth with ice, pop like minimalist sculptures against a crystalline sky. A thin fiber of cloud wafts high. It's the world's most perfecto ribbon of smoke, as if I were a smoker, as if ribbons of breath, of nothing, could mean anything as I go back to the frigid real world.

We pass the ass-side of the BFI and see his supports, how he's propped up. From this angle you can see the chief is hollow. He puts on a fierce face, but he's more air than substance. We travel under the influence of really good coffee to the sounds of early Aimee Mann. "I know where this boat will go/ Pulled down by the undertow/ It's lucky I know / How to row."

Her lyrics are so very clever. I can't think of a single thing to say that is half as sharp. I am blunt.

"FedEx picks up at Mom's office," Noah says, pausing the music between tracks. "If you want to, drop your applications there. If it's easier." He drums his fingers on the steering wheel, a second hand marking the time I have left. Tick. Good. Tick. Bye.

"Got it covered," I say, cranking Aimee again.

Noah deposits me at the mouth of Exchange Street, my Beans booty in hand—and my actual Beans boots, my prezzie to myself, on my content feet.

"Don't be late," he says from a rolled-down window. In the cold air, his words sound sharp, prickled.

The ferry sits in the blinding morning light where the water meets the road. So photogenic, it's like a view from a movie, except it's my view, my movie.

I turn, expecting to see Noah waggling his head to the music, waiting for me to board. But he is off.

The sight of his thin pale exhaust is what does me in. A good thing I have on my new supercapable boots. At least I can put one dicey foot in front of the other.

On board, Henry coils a yellow swath of rope, and I wish, for a brief cold minute, that his hands were snaking through mine. I give him a little windshield-wiper wave—not a big commitment.

A pink bakery box sits solo on top of his folded fleece. I peek: lemon. There are no regular cars this morning—just a lone cement truck. I'm not really hungry, but why waste a good cupcake?

As the ferry pushes off from solid ground to the sway of water, I'm bowled over by a whiff of redfish, a truly stinkpot bait, wafting up from the metal floor.

Think: This would be an inspired boarding school question. Tell us what the sea smells like. This is the true test of an original mind, a student who can plumb her senses.

Think: It's a layered smell. A cup of miso soup, a goblet of Clorox, a splash of swampy rocks, a water-warped paperback, too much salt on french fries.

Think: Here's why Maine is different from Santa Monica, the hometown of Mother Maris. It's too sunny there. It makes my eyes hurt. And it's too easy. It takes zippo work to get to the beach. No cutting of feet on sharp-tongued rocks.

This is something to love about this place, about my place in this place. Out comes the lobster folder. I lean against the crusted-out bumper of the cement mixer and face dreaded question number one, the first for last, the first thing they will read about me.

Sloppy copy:

What I like most about myself is my geography. I like the view on my island—at least the view looking out. Once you get used to seeing a wide-open sky, even something as pretty as the cobble-stone streets of Portland have a way of narrowing the vista.

I like how everything fits on an island. How the houses sit on the ledge, and the ledge sits on the inlet. How everyone, every structure, clusters together. How the wind whistles into Crescent Cove when the tide is just right.

Useless knowledge: The islands in Casco Bay are called, collectively, the Calendar Isles—based on the (bogus) fact that there are 365 of them. Even if you count every ledge, the real number is closer to 100. I can promise you I will tell the truth about my island, my geography, my family, myself if you find room for me at your fine institution. Truth in topography—I'll even start a club if you want.

Here's a true fact. Winslow Homer painted his famous sea portraits just down the beach at Prouts Neck. (His studio is open for tours, by the way—just give a ring.) Homer was brilliant, but for me, the sea isn't about seeing.

I like to shut my eyes and listen to the slurp of the waves. The sound drowns out my own clattery thoughts. It's like those big spiral shells, the type you hold to your ear to supposedly hear the ocean. Those shells don't land in Maine, at least not in one piece. Here we get crumbles. Here, if you want to hear the sea, you have to be outside. There is no way to listen secondhand.

Mental bookmark: If and when I leave the land of lobsters, I will bid on those spiral shells on eBay. A pair—so I can dream in stereo. Even right now, right out here in the middle of the bay that houses my home, I already miss this place. I already miss myself.

Five (b)

Boom, boom, boom, we dock. Henry gives a random townie and her kid a hand getting off. I hang back and crack my toes inside my roomy boots.

"See you tonight?" I mean to come off confident.

"You never know," he says.

No, I never do. Did I misunderstand the cupcake overture? Does he try to brush-kiss every island inmate?

As much as I miss Fern, the frond, and Eb, the brother, I'm not quite ready to walk through the door and be their Charlotte. Instead I sit at the ferry bench and see the view, my movie view, from this angle. The trees hugging the coast wear snow garlands—the real thing, not the kind from Wal-Mart. It's too pretty to feel self-pity.

With my new favorite footwear, I kick at pieces of stone underfoot. The ground is rock-solid frozen. It won't give. The sky, however, has turned the perfect fluid blue. I think it's called Rayleigh scattering, but

Libby would know for sure. I see one single contrail 30,000 feet above. United 245 from JFK to Istanbul. I'm making this up, but it could be true. Passengers are soaring overhead, oblivious to the idea that life goes on beneath the obvious.

"I have shells in my pocket," I hear from behind.

I whip around. Strands of hair catch in my mouth.

A lanky frame fills my personal viewfinder. Who's that? I think for a millisecond before realizing: Dad. It's my father, and he has come clean, very clean. Clean clothes, clean-shaven. He's younger and older without his beard.

Fern holds the handles of the stroller with both fists, and Eb has Gussy's leash on his lap. Gussy herself sits with perfect poodle posture.

"I'm heading home," I say, letting my hair cover up my face. Our hirsute roles are suddenly reversed.

"Well, we're heading to you. Collected a few welcome-home presents along the way." He hands over a dismal bunch of shells.

"They're broken."

"Six-letter word: *lamina*—shell with a thin plate of rock." His smile spreads from corner to corner, like a slice of cantaloupe. Maybe he always smiled like that, maybe his happiness was just buried by fuzz.

"I like my present." The presence of shells, the non-presence of facial hair.

Dad strokes his smooth face. "It's cold. But we'll see how it goes."

"Miss me?" I ask Fern.

"A little, actually," she says and then turns to push Eb up the hill.

As we round the corner of home, I have to squint. The sun glares off a large shiny spot in the front.

Gone one day and Dad has transformed not just himself but the whole fugging yard. On what was once a patchy lawn, he has built a skating rink, a big frozen ice cube.

"Having a Gretzky moment?" I ask, sliding my mittie across the utterly unmarred ice.

"Been scheming," he says. "Finished yesterday, the kids and I," he says, gesturing to the children as if he is introducing them to me.

Away twenty-four hours and already it's "the kids and I." Already I'm a goner.

"We used buckets from your tub!" Fern says. She pushes Eb in the stroller on the ice. A sleigh-of-hand.

"*Pourquoi?*"

"Why not?" Mr. Bolt-from-the-Blue says, again with the melon smile. "Noah or the neighbors can come slap a hockey puck around."

I can't keep Noah out of the conversation—or out of my front yard. "You don't even talk to the neighbors."

"Not true. Just not Kat." He nods his beanied head toward her garden. "Your mother can't abide her. For whatever reason."

Because he shtups her. I could pick at that scab. Instead I pick at another. "This will melt at the first thaw."

"Not so, Debbie Doubter. Should hold until spring, or at least Passover, which is early this year."

Fern oh-so-carefully parks Eb off the ice and locks his stroller wheels in place, as I would. She spins with her arms stretched up to the still transcendent blue sky. Eb is transfixed. He looks up to her. Fern clears her throat. "Ladies and gentlemen, take my advice. Pull down your pants and slide on the ice," she says, quoting an old Yankee recess rhyme now banned on the Mainland. Already changing the status quo.

I hold out my hands to catch a flurry, but there's really no new snow. It's just a few random flakes drifting from the trees. "What if you're wrong? What if you're flat-out fucking wrong?" I ask Dad.

"Whoa, has your mother's mouth come home?"

"Has it?"

"Well, if I am wrong, big deal. We'll put in the old Jew canoe and paddle." The reference to the Canoe of Jew—a wooden Beans model from Dad's days as a camp counselor in the Berkshires—brings back tippy summer memories.

Guess Mom and her mouth are still MIA. I sit down on the ice and splay my legs, like Gussy in her most indecent pose. The ground is so slidy. "Can I play hooky? Hockey? Hooky?" I ask.

Quick mental math: The 3:52 ferry will give me plenty of time to deliver the apps to FedEx on the Maineland by the magic five o'clock deadline.

Dad tosses me his beanie. "I'll call you in sick." Hell, I'll call us all in sick.

My just-hatched-now plan is to finish the app paperwork right after lunch. First, though, I need to enjoy my hooky, or what is the point? I dig through the mudroom in search of my rusty skates. My feet haven't grown since sixth grade—no lie. I sit on the checkerboard floor and pull the left lace so tight it threatens to break. I can't wait for my ankles to ache.

By the time I'm ready, everyone else has gone in. That's okay do-kay.

On the virgin ice, my first circle is speculative, but then I get my feet under me and pick up speed. I'm skimming on water, when you think about it, hydroplaning on frozen vodka, enjoying a microclimate where the only sounds I hear are my skates sluicing through a lens of frost. A nearby hemlock shudders, shaking snow off its limb-shoulders. It's a brilliant morning.

Five (c)

The water is at a rolling boil, ready for lunch, for pasta for four. The rude ring of the phone interrupts the peace of the kitchen.

I don't pick up. I can't imagine who I'd want on the other end. Dad doesn't move either. Maybe he's not keen on another mystery-girl conversation.

Fern finally answers. "She's here, actually. We'll see you soon," she says, handing me the receiver.

"Charlotte?" the jagged voice of Maris asks. She's too loud. "I forgot my book. Look up the number of Marco for me. I need highlights. Marco will be under S, remember. For Salon."

"Are you still in New York? Can't you find a phone book?"

"I don't appreciate your insolence. I like to think I can rely on my family when needed." In color emergencies— that part went unsaid. And who is the unreliable one, exactly? That part went unsaid too.

Her red book is where it should be (junk drawer), even if she is not where she should be (Bleak). I read the number slowly. For some reason, I want to keep her on the phone.

"My appreciation," she yells over a passing bus or something. "You have been a help." Then she stops talking. Another bus zooms by.

Why is she the one staying on the phone now that she has what she wants? I hang up and let her go. My stomach crunches together—hunger or hurt, who knows.

I drain the linguini and toss it with pesto (the sauce, not the fabricated language of my childhood).

"Can you serve?" I ask Dad. "I've lost my appetite. Besides, got some stuff to finish. Upstairs."

He nods and shaves a few perfect curls off a block of Parmesan cheese.

In the peace of my blue womb with a view, I go into hyperfocus/fuck-us mode. It takes all twenty-four tracks of the original *Tommy*—all hail the Who—and then, *voilà*, I am *fini*. I've typed all my crazy thoughts into stiff and proper MLA English. I spell-check twice (catch a T-shit reference) before I print the final essays.

Then I gather together the many pieces of me—teacher recs, test scores, transcript, photo, and hot-off-the-printer essays—and skip down my clifflike attic steps.

Even though I'm wearing a cute skirt, I go practical with the footwear and tug on my sure Beans boots—no fug-me heels today.

Time check: Thirty-seven minutes until I have to leave for the fateful ferry, the boat that will deliver me and my paperwork to the high priest of FedEx.

At the kitchen table, Dad sits with Fern making a paper-bag puppet. Eb is on his lap, clapping for no reason.

"Say 'Charlotte,'" I say, putting my freckles in front of Eb. If he can say my name it's an omen. At this moment—as the air begins to bite into dusk and the light slants across the kitchen like an outstretched arm—I want someone to ask me to stay, even if I decide to put one boot in front of the other and go.

"Dadadd," he says.

I sit and slip my hands under my ass so I won't get lost in puppet-making. "I've got an errand to run," I say.

"Could you be a little more explicit?" Dad asks.

"Well, I could. So could you, for that matter. Mr. Plaid Man."

"Whoa, I'm lost," he says.

"I'm talking about your criminal plaid shirt," I say, with an astoundingly even voice.

"I thought we were, you were, on to something else. My plaid shirt?" he asks, raising his bushy (singular) brow. "The one you've been modeling?"

I nod to Fern. "Take Eb out to see if the rink has turned into a puddle yet. I'll be right there."

"I'm there, you're here," she says.

"I'm here, you're there." I give her a hug—a desperate squeeze, actually—and zip Eb into his snowzy suit.

Time check to ferry push-off: twenty-four minutes.

I face Dad and tightly link my pinkies together like I'm about to launch into an idiotic Israeli folk dance. "The shirt was on that *America's Top Ten Wanted* show." On *show*, of all words, my voice cracks. Only now do I notice he wears another, drabber plaid. The last thing in the world he needs is one more feeble tartan. What was I thinking, buying him a new Beans model and aiding and abetting his crime, fashionwise and/or otherwise?

He strokes his nonexistent beard. "I didn't know I was in the picture."

"What did you do? If you don't tell me, I will call Nana. I will do a DMV search. I will see why you're wanted—for armed robbery or destruction of federal property or for dealing meth on the ferry, for all I know." I sound breakable.

Gussy runs in circles, chasing her elusive tail.

"Being open," he says slowly, "is overrated."

I walk over to the shut-tight window with a winter view of the water. I push up from the bottom and feel it give. I open my mouth. I crave a breeze, a sign of life. When it comes, the cold catches in the back of my throat. It's salty; it's a pickle. "What happened to living in an open society?" I ask.

"Very nice, throwing that back at me. What do you really want to know? What are you most dying to know?" To look at him, I have to look down. He sips his tea and holds the cup to his lips for fourteen seconds. I count.

"Don't pull a Mom and tell me everything," I say when he finally returns cup to saucer.

"Interesting. What did Mom say?"

"Too much. Say less, but tell me something. Enough so I don't hate you."

"Ask me. One great question. Nine letters: catechize."

"You're Jewish, Dad."

"I haven't been your father forever. I had a life before you, for many, many years before you. Ask."

"Have you done anything illegal?" I breathe in so tightly my nostrils nearly close up. Whatever he answers, I am in this alone.

"Driving without a license, drinking underage. Same as you."

"That you regret? Anything you deeply regret?"

We lock eyes. Brown irises dominate blue. He is recessive (ha!). "There are transgressions. Of course there are transgressions. Not excessive. One or two more than the average dad," he says. He pushes his cheek out with his tongue.

"Stop with the tongue dance," I say.

"The beard used to hide it. It's my nervous tic," he says. "Like your leg. No one is going to show up at the house in the middle of the night to take me away, if that's what you're afraid of." He gives his cheek a little knock. "Or is that what you were wishing? You can have another question. Fire away."

"Who's the girl? The pale girl?" Referring to her as Pale Chick seems too intimate. Like I've spent hours obsessed with her. Which, of course, I have.

"Charlotte is an old friend."

"Charlotte?" Did he really say Charlotte? "Charlotte is my name." I close my eyes and rearrange my letters. I am Clatter. Torah. Earth. Threat. Late. Rat. Heart.

"Yes, first love, real love. Charlotte was my Noah."

I rest for a second on just how nimbly Dad has nailed what Noah is to me, I am to him. "How do you know?"

"I know, Charlotte. We are family. We are alike."

"You named me after a criminal?" My voice fractures. It betrays me, and I don't care. I finger the seaglass necklace Fern made me—it's flipped around so I can't find the groove. "What about Fern and Eb? Are they criminal names too? Or lying names?" My fingers twitch, and my wrist starts to whisk a phantom bakery item. I walk across to the pantry and take a can of organic blueberries off the shelf. I might make a crumble. Or I might just crumple.

"You aren't named for anyone. The name is yours," Dad says. "Though Maris does love E. B. White, no doubt about that. She, of course, assumes you are that Charlotte of the spider species." He shrugs and puts his hands up. "As your mother would say, so sue me."

My voice is preternaturally (Wordly Wise Word!) calm. "Answer this with your hands down, please. Why is that Charlotte wanted? And tell me if you're wanted too."

He lowers his palms. I flinch in the hush. "Charlotte bombed a car. It was parked near the gate of a nuclear plant. Not here, not even close. In eastern Washington. The plant was decommissioned—no danger there. The car was supposed to be empty—no danger there either. Charlotte was making a point about the lust for profit. The bomb was packed with one-dollar bills, and it was just supposed to ravage this gas-gulping Lincoln owned by some multinational firm." Randomly, he spreads his fingers wide on the table. At Thanksgiving, I traced around Fern's stretched-wide fingers to make turkey-shaped place cards before we visited Maris in the psych ward. "Except it wasn't empty, the car. There was some-one in the backseat. One of our group, actually. A sweet, shy girl from the UK. She died." He says this quietly, but I don't ask him to repeat it.

"Is that supposed to make it better? That you're in love with an assassin. An eco-assassin, but a killer all the same." I have the instinct to bolt right now. Time check: fifteen minutes to go. I hurl my backpack over my shoulder.

"Wait," Dad says, holding up his hand like a stop sign. "You asked the questions, now stay for the answers. One, I am not in love with a murderess. No more. I grew up. And, two, I am not wanted. No one wants me. Not anymore."

He glances out the window. I follow his gaze out the glass, toward Kat's house, then look back just to him. "Do you mean the FBI? Or do you mean Mom or me?" I ask.

"All of the above. My energy, my activism, goes to making a life on the island. And to Scrabble—a little joke there."

"So you're innocent?" I ask. That's the multi-national, multirational question.

"Innocent of what? Once you know something about someone, you can't unremember it. You can't put it back in the box."

I think of his sweet-smelling wooden box and walk over and hold his fingers. He's cold. I wish I could slide his icy hands through an airport screening machine. To see if he wired a bomb or fondled a gun or loved Mom or held me. To x-ray his soul—and, by proxy, my own.

Out of the blue(berry) I say, "You showed me yours. I'll show you mine. If you want to know." I grab my lobster folder and offer it up like a homemade pie.

His tongue is once again visibly in cheek. "I know," he says. "Didn't you wonder why they arrived addressed to you in the first place?"

"No. NO. I didn't." I consider going to the window and grabbing a crispy breath of air. But I can't. The gravity surrounding the kitchen chair is suddenly very strong—strengthened by surprise and something like gratitude. "I hadn't wondered at all, not of all the things I had wondered about," I add.

"I called admission offices and faxed them your PSAT. Now that you're the Charlotte who may leave, I'm almost sorry. Almost."

I lean over and kiss his forehead, holding my lips against his smooth skin until I feel his vein pulse. My lip gloss leaves a sticky spot.

"You made me shiny." He holds up a dish towel but doesn't wipe off the pink.

"And you're okay with me going in the fall? And Maris? Will she be okay?"

"Maris will be Maris, and the rest of us will be fine. First-rate. And it might be sooner. These places may well have spring openings. It's your choice."

"We're all so pro-choice. Mom filled me in about the

abortion." I regressively bite the collar of my T-shit/
shirt. I leave a wet blotch.

"Ah," he says. "She's been in that kind of soul-
cleansing mood of late. Well, pro-choice is more interesting and more complicated than that. I'm choosing
to stay on the island—for now. And to stay with your
mother—for now."

"Do you think she prefers that other island, the
island of Manhattan?"

"That's possible. But wherever she is, you can
choose to leave. Let's say you can be the first," the un-
Unabomber says. His eyes are clammy.

"Time to fish or cut bait—or whatever a bumblefuck
local would say."

"Nice to have the sharp Charlotte back."

I head to the door and, because I'm me, divert to
thinking of doorknobs. Making a choice means not
only opening a door but walking through. I'm good at
looking at doors. At scrutinizing the hinges and con-
demning the colors. But actually turning the knob
(brass or bronze or pewter or chrome) and commit-
ting to a future I've actually chosen. Well, that's a whole
new concept.

I squint at my watch, afraid I've wasted time. But I'm
okay if I hurry.

"Go," Dad says.

Five (d)

I cross the threshold from the tangerine light of the kitchen to the twilight-skied outside. Now, eleven minutes to make the nine-minute walk. Two minutes to fritter.

At the edge of the ice-rink, Fern has her mitts on Eb's stroller. "See you later, skater," I say, unbuckling the boy and airlifting him out by his armpits for a quick kiss. This is maturity. I resist the easy joke (he ain't heavy; he's my brother) even though he's both.

"See you later, skater," Fern repeats, waving good-bye to Eb.

"Fern, stay with Dad." She starts to follow. "Stay," I say very softly. Gussy sits, for once following directions, even though they're not meant for her.

"Come, kids," Dad says, turning camp-counselory. "Let's go on a hunt for the trusty bread machine and make a challah—attempt to."

"Save me," I say, returning Eb to Fern's parka arms. "Save me a hunk."

"Use Dr. Cole's shortcut," he says. "Run."

I do—with my apps clutched to my chest and my honest-to-Beans boots biting into the compacted snow. I sprint past Chloe's house, past Kat's garden, past the library and kayak rental (summers only), and make a sharp left into Dr. Cole's yard.

There, where there should be a straight shot through to Ocean Road, is a large pile of wood. It appears Dr. Cole/Cold had a cord, actually two cords, delivered before the storm. The logs are stacked between the birches, smack in my way. Up and over is the only choice. But even with my appropriate footwear, I don't want to risk getting my apps wet. Or my striped tights. Or my short skirt that un-pianofies my legs.

I quickly U-turn to take the lesser road, the narrow bike lane that Susannah and I pedal down seventeen times a day in summer. But something weird happens. I can't find the path. Yesterday's fourteen inches of fresh flakes seem to have amalgamated right here, swirling and rearranging the landscape. Which of the many white-mounded shrubs mark the entrance? I lose my know-how, my snow-how. I spin slowly in a circle, a disco ball looking for my bearings. It turns out I can get lost on an island, after all.

There's no choice but to charge back to Dr. Cole and hurdle. "If you're going to tramp through my yard, at least know where the hell you're going," the good doctor bellows from his sentry-post at the front door.

"I can explain," I say, scaling the pile. "But I don't have time." The logs wriggle and fidget under me, like my leg tic supersized. "I'll restack later."

"Yes, you will," he shouts.

"Apologies," I say, hoping I don't sound ironic.

Without even stopping to brush the snow off, I tear down to the dock in record time.

At least I think I do. But I'm wrong. Once again, mistaken.

Because at the crest of the hill, I hear the dreaded air horn. The bleat sounds like the long, loud cry I wish I could force out of my frozen throat.

The sun slides into the horizon. Henry and the ferry—backlit very nicely, by the way—pull away without me. Henry gives a shruggy wave.

Welcome to the debris field that is my life. The next ferry arrives in Portland too late for the FedEx pickup, and the b.s. paperwork clearly states "no late applications will be considered."

"Shit," I yell. No. One. Is. There. It is too silent.

"Shit, shit."

That's forty-five times in case anyone is counting. My former good-luck number, the number that guarantees an aircraft won't crash, now crashes down on me. Along with my plans to make a new and boundless life.

I'm here. They're here. We're all right fucking here.

For some number of minutes I sit on the bench and watch the water on the move through the cracks in the dock boards. The water is going somewhere, but not me. I lost my choice/chance. Delta 8303 from Logan to Uzbekistan is overhead. It might be—why the hell not?

The sky is divided in two—night on top, dwindling dusk below. It is, finally, officially, the Solstice. I put myself on the flight, imagine using the nose of the plane as a paintbrush, dipping and blending to merge the two skies together.

Then I snap out of it because I am stuck, fixed on the cold, slick ground. I look around for someone to kayak me over—in the summer I'd have no trouble talking my way into a ride.

Norma, the fartacular cashier, comes down the hill, cigarette in hand. The fresh cold air neutralizes her various odors. "Got in a new granola—currant. Put some aside for you," she says.

"Taking a granola holiday," I say. The thought of cereal makes me surreally ill.

I suppose I could just go home and swirl around the ice with Fern, teach Eb to say my name, discover the art of baking challah. I suppose I could just force myself to enjoy, at least endure, one more year in Lobsterland.

I take off my parka to feel the air, to feel alive. The breeze slaps my cheeks, lips. My arms are free to swing.

I turn back to the hill, waiting for my mood to catch up with my brain.

The thrum of the phantom plane gets louder in my ears. I turn and look up at a big rip in the sky. Nothing. It's gone. Uzbekistan without me. I can't even leave in a fantasy. I shiver and throw my coat over my shoulders. It's seven degrees—what was I thinking?

My eyes follow the sky down into the water. And then I see it coming. The noise is not above, but out to sea.

The tail wag of a wake. Out of the blue, the ferry circles back into view. Here comes my second choice/chance.

Henry bobs into the dock, no air horn. He doesn't do a full-on stop. The engine idles.

I charge back down the gentle hill, sure-footed. My coat flaps behind me. I slip my arms back through the sleeves and pat the pocket where my apps are now carefully creased. Even without the horn, the air seems more energetic, less empty. The smells—diesel, beer, pine, peanuts, wet dog—are the smells of optimism.

I take the measure of the jump and *jeté* on board.

"Thank you. So much," I shout over the engine.

"Look at that. Charlotte is being nice," Henry says. He comes nose to nose with me. His fennel toothpaste wafts through the icy air. "I could never get away with a turnaround in the summer. But the nine people on this boat don't give a whoop. I told them it would score me big points with you."

I bust out a laugh. A giggle at first—like "oh, you're sweet." Then loud. Then louder, like I'm pushing out every last gasp uphill.

We coast past the boathouse, which will soon throw open its doors for the Solstice dance, for the coupling of my bestish friend with my formerish boyfriend, the love of my life—past tense, past perfect tense.

White Christmas lights twinkle around the windows. Susannah herself is visible in her street clothes, waltzing through the snow-flecked street with a garbage bag shielding her Lobster gown from the mist. Noah bounces behind with bags of accoutrement. He's already in his Lennon-like suit, and he looks great— freshly pressed and fizzy. Here it is, the actual Solstice, the official dead of winter. And yet it's not dark, as in depressing. There is happiness all around.

As the boat churns forward, I pull Henry, the unboyfriend, toward me and kiss him without a blink of restraint. I want to take our breath(s) away. There is now one sky. Half of me knows I should stay here, where I recognize every inch of land and inches, fathoms possibly, of sea.

The ferry sways, heavy as a keg, but I feel buoyant. Because a slightly bigger half knows that there are other places where the water is deep and clear and interesting. Where life begins.